Witch Is How Life Changed Forever

Chapter 1

Sometimes, being a witch was brilliant.

I'd just arrived in Washbridge when the heavens decided to open, and it began to pour with rain. When I checked my bag, there was no sign of my umbrella. What an idiot I was; I must have left it on the hallstand.

I took a quick look around, to make sure no one was watching and then magicked myself to the office building. Yes, I know I'm not supposed to use magic in the human world for selfish reasons, but come on, it was raining cats and dogs. You didn't really expect me to get soaked to the skin, did you?

In the outer office, Mrs V was standing next to the linen basket in which she stored her yarn. Grumbling away to herself, she had her back to the door, and hadn't even noticed I was there.

"Good morning, Mrs V."

"Oh, good morning, Jill. I didn't see you come in."

"Is something wrong?"

"Yes, I'd say so. Most of my yarn is ruined. Absolutely ruined."

"Don't tell me that Winky got in there again."

"No, I can't blame the cat this time. The basket appears to have been infested with something."

"*Infested*?" I shuddered. "With what?" I walked over so I could take a closer look.

"At least half of it is unusable," she said. "Look, when you pick the balls up, they fall apart in your hands."

"What could have caused that?"

"I have no idea. I expected to find some kind of creepy-crawly, but there's no sign of any. This is a complete disaster. I've promised to knit something for a number of people, and I don't know how I'm going to manage now."

"Couldn't you just order some more?"

"I can try, but some of the colours are quite rare. And then there's the question of whether it's still safe to keep yarn in the basket. For all I know, whatever did this might still be around somewhere."

There wasn't anything I could do or say to help, so I left Mrs V to it, and went through to my office where I found Winky, dressed to the nines.

"Where are you going?"

"Nowhere."

"So why are you dressed up like a dog's dinner, then?"

"*Dog's*? Do you mind?"

"You know what I mean. What's with the whistle and flute?"

"Hark at you with your cockney rhyming slang. I never would have Adam and Eve'd it."

"Are we really doing this?"

"You bet. Just take a butcher's at my ones and twos."

"Enough already. Are you going to tell me why you're all dressed up or not?"

"Don't tell me you've forgotten? It's the national finals of the best dressed cat competition a week on Wednesday. I'm trying on a few new outfits for size."

"You're not seriously going through with that, are you?"

"Of course I am. There's five thousand pounds at stake. I am, without a shadow of a doubt, the best dressed cat in the country, so why wouldn't I?"

"Is the competition open to male and female cats?"

"Of course, but they're run on separate nights."

"Where's it going to be held?"

"In London, of course."

"And how are you getting down there?"

"Funny you should ask."

"Forget it. I'm not driving you all the way to London."

"Come on, Jill. You wouldn't want me to miss out on such a prestigious event, would you?"

"What's in it for me?"

He thought about it for a moment. "I'll give you twenty percent of my prize money."

"What if you don't win anything?"

"Of course I'll win. It's a foregone conclusion. Come on. Twenty percent is one thousand pounds."

"And all I have to do is drive you down there, wait until it's over, and then bring you back home again?"

"Yeah, that's it."

"I don't have to come into the competition with you?"

"Not if you don't want to."

"I don't."

"What do you say, then? It's easy money."

Jack and I were low on funds, so the thousand pounds would definitely come in handy. I could drop Winky off at the competition, have a little walk around London, pick up something to eat, and then take him home again.

"Okay, I'll do it."

"Thanks, Jill. You won't regret it."

***

My first appointment of the week was with a Mr and Mrs Kramer. He had what you might call a lived-in face.

His wife looked at least ten years younger than him.

I knew from the brief telephone conversation I'd had with Mrs Kramer that their son, Arnold, was in prison after being convicted of murder.

"Thank you for seeing us, Mrs Maxwell," Mrs Kramer said.

"Please call me Jill. You mentioned on the phone that your son was in prison."

"That's right. He's been there for almost five years now, and we're becoming more and more concerned about his health, aren't we, Randolph?"

"Indeed." Mr Kramer nodded. "He really doesn't look well at all."

"When was the last time you saw him?"

"Monday of last week. He barely spoke to us all the time we were with him. He's become a shadow of his former self, and we're worried that he might do something silly."

"Have you mentioned this to the authorities at the prison?"

"Yes, and they've promised to keep an eye on him, but the only thing that's really going to help is to get him out of there. That's why we're here today."

"Why don't you start by telling me about the murder that your son was convicted of."

The two of them looked at one another, as though they were trying to decide who should tell the story. Eventually, it was Mrs Kramer who did so. "Arnold was working in a fast food restaurant. It's the one out of town on Washbridge Westway, near to the roundabout."

"I think I know the one you mean."

"It's actually changed hands since he worked there, and

is now called Wash Burgers, but it's still in the same location. He was serving at the drive-thru hatch that particular night. Arnold had been seeing a young woman named Alison Reed."

"Is that relevant to the murder in some way?"

"Yes. It was Alison who was murdered."

"I see. Sorry, please carry on."

"Alison was Arnold's first serious girlfriend. He'd been so excited when they got together, but unfortunately it didn't work out. He wouldn't tell us the ins and outs of why it had ended, but I got the impression that she'd been seeing someone else behind his back."

"Just so I'm clear. How long before the night of her murder had their relationship ended?"

"A few weeks before. On that particular night, Alison had gone to the drive-thru to order food, and it was Arnold who served her. Later that same night, her body was found in her car; she'd been poisoned. Traces of the poison that killed her were found in the food which she'd purchased from the drive-thru. They said that Arnold had administered the poison, but that's complete nonsense."

"How had he taken the breakup of their relationship?"

"He was devastated, but that doesn't mean he wanted to hurt Alison. He's not that kind of boy. He certainly would never have killed her."

"What other evidence did the prosecution produce in court?"

"One of the witnesses, a friend of Alison Reed, testified that she'd seen Arnold threaten Alison. And worst of all, they found traces of the poison that killed Alison at the house Arnold shared."

"What did he have to say about that?"

"He denies ever threatening Alison, and he has always maintained that he has no idea how the poison got there."

"How many people shared the house with Arnold?"

"Just one other: A young man called Roy Sissons. I believe he still lives there. Do you think you'll be able to help us to prove his innocence, Jill?"

"I'll certainly try, but I'll need to spend a little time doing my own research on the case first. After I've done that, I'd like to talk to you again, this time at your house. Would that be possible?"

"Of course."

The Kramers were in slightly higher spirits when they left. In truth, though, I wasn't overly optimistic that I was going to be able to clear their son's name. The fact that the police had found traces of the poison, which had killed Alison Reed, on the food that Arnold had served to her, and at his house, really wasn't good.

I was about to place the paperwork for this new case in a folder, but when I checked the drawer for a paperclip, the tray was empty. I could have sworn there were dozens the last time I looked.

Just then, the temperature in the room dropped, and I could sense that a ghost was about to make an appearance. Winky must have sensed it too because he shot under the sofa. I assumed it would be my Mum or Dad, or even the colonel or Priscilla. In fact, it turned out to be Madge and Lily from the bridge club in GT.

"Hello, you two. This is a surprise."

"I hope you don't mind our dropping in on you like this, Jill," Madge said.

"Of course not. Won't you take a seat?"

"No, thanks." Lily shook her head. "We can't stay for long. We just wanted to drop by, to say thank you for what you did."

"It was my pleasure. I'm just glad that Selina and her boyfriend have been brought to book. It was bad enough that they stole the jewellery, but to then try and sell it to your surviving relatives. That was downright despicable. Has everyone got their jewellery back?"

"It's all been returned now," Lily said. "Apart from that which had already been sold to a surviving relative of course. But at least we know that's in good hands."

"I have some other exciting news, Jill," Madge said. "I'm now in contact with Cynthia."

"Your daughter? That's fantastic. I'm surprised because when I spoke to her, she seemed very sceptical about the afterlife."

"After what you told me about the reception she'd given you, I didn't hold out much hope, but I figured it was worth one last try to contact her. And it worked."

"That's brilliant."

"I think that your little chat with her must have sown a seed of doubt in her mind. Whatever the reason, she heard my voice when I called to her. She was a little shocked at first. Scared even. But once she'd got over that, everything was okay. We've spoken a few times since then."

"I'm so very happy for you, Madge."

"I can't thank you enough, Jill. I know I originally came to you because of the missing jewellery, but being reunited with Cynthia is far more valuable to me than jewellery could ever be."

After Madge and Lily had left, I did some initial research on the Kramer case. What I discovered was pretty much in line with what the Kramers had told me.

On that fateful night, Alison Reed had called at what was then known as The Burger Barn; a drive-thru on the Washbridge Westway roundabout. It had been her ex-boyfriend, Arnold Kramer, who had served her. That much was not in dispute because the exchange had been caught on CCTV.

Alison Reed's body had been found later that same evening in her car, which was parked outside her apartment. One of her neighbours had walked by the car and noticed that Alison had her head pressed up against the windscreen. In her phone call to the police, the woman had told them that Alison was unresponsive, and she thought she might be dead.

The post-mortem would later reveal that Alison had died from poisoning. The substance that had killed her was some kind of rat poison. Forensic investigations had revealed that there were traces of that same poison on the burger that Alison had partially consumed. Having established that there had once been a relationship between Arnold and Alison, the police soon identified him as their prime suspect.

Two days later, Arnold's housemate had contacted the police because his cat had died after eating poison. It was soon established that the poison, which had killed the cat, was the same one that had been used to murder Alison.

Right from the start, Arnold Kramer had insisted that he was innocent. Although he admitted he'd felt bitter for the way Alison had treated him, he denied killing her. Arnold insisted he knew nothing about the poison, but he could offer no explanation for how it came to be on the food or at his house.

It was clear this was not going to be an easy case. The evidence was all stacked against Arnold, and it wasn't difficult to see why the jury had convicted him.

"Hey, Jill." Winky held up his phone. "Do you want to see something hilarious?"

"If it's a photo of my decoupage, I've already told you to take that down."

"Nah, it's not that. This is much funnier."

"Go on, then. I could do with a good laugh."

He jumped off the sofa, and onto my desk.

"Just take a look at this." He passed me his phone.

"Where did you get that photo?"

"They've definitely captured your nose."

"I asked where you got the photo of my waxwork from?"

"I have my sources."

"But the museum is in the paranormal world."

"So? I have contacts there too. Is that waxwork really on view for the public to see?"

"At the moment, yes. But not for much longer if I have anything to do with it."

"You should get them to make small replicas of it and bring one into the office. Every time I'm feeling a bit down, I could look at that, and it would be guaranteed to cheer me up."

"No chance." I grabbed his phone.

"Hey, what are you doing with that? You can't throw it through the—"

"Whoops. Sorry, it just slipped out of my hand."

Chapter 2

Winky had disappeared out of the window, presumably in search of his phone. I'd done all the research I could for one day on the Kramer case, and I needed a break, so I magicked myself over to Aunt Lucy's house.

"Hi, Jill." She was busy dusting the ornaments in the lounge.

"Are you okay, Aunt Lucy? You look a little tired."

"To tell you the truth, I haven't slept well for the last couple of nights."

"Lester hasn't been eating apples recently, has he?"

"Apples?" She looked somewhat puzzled by the question. "No, I don't think so. He is rather partial to the occasional peach, though. Why do you ask?"

"No reason. How come you haven't been sleeping very well?"

"Our new neighbours have had their baby. He's a lovely little boy. Well, not so little actually. He certainly has a fine pair of lungs on him."

"The baby woke you up?"

"Not exactly. When he starts to cry, it sets Barry off howling. He's the one who wakes me up. I've tried telling him that it's only a little baby, and there's nothing to howl about. But, well, you know how Barry can be."

"A bit dim, you mean?"

"I wouldn't have put it quite so harshly. But yes."

"If you'd like to go and get your head down, I can always call back later."

"Don't be silly. I'm pleased for an excuse to take a break. The dust will still be here later. Why don't we go and have a cup of tea? You never know, it might wake me up a little." We went through to the kitchen where Aunt Lucy put on the kettle, and then walked over to the cupboard. "You're in luck, Jill. I bought a new packet of custard creams yesterday."

"You don't happen to have any ginger nuts, do you?"

"Instead of custard creams?"

"Yeah. I really fancy a ginger nut right now."

"I never thought I'd see the day when you refused a custard cream."

"Neither did I. Perhaps I've just had too many over the years, and now it's caught up with me."

"You're in luck. I do have a packet of ginger nuts."

As we were chatting over a cuppa, I heard the sound of paws on the stairs. Moments later, Barry came charging into the room.

"Hello, big guy, how are you?"

"Hi, Jill." He rested his paws on my knees. "I'm fine, thanks, but I'm very busy." He turned to Aunt Lucy and said, "What would you like me to do now, Lucy?"

"I think you've done everything, Barry."

"There must be something else I can do. Shall I tidy the bedroom again?"

"Okay, if you must."

And with that, he started for the door.

"Barry, hold on a minute. Aunt Lucy tells me you've taken to howling in the night."

"I have to keep the beebee away."

"The what?"

"Lucy said the beebee are next door. I don't want them to come around here and attack us in our sleep."

"No, Barry, you've got the wrong end of the—"

It was too late because he'd already gone charging back upstairs.

"Why is he so keen to help out all of a sudden?" I said.

"Dolly took it upon herself to enrol him in the Dog Scouts." Aunt Lucy sighed. "He absolutely loves it, but they've told him that he has to help around the house every day. He's been driving me crazy."

"Still, it must be nice to have the help."

"Normally, I'd say yes, but it usually ends up with me having more work to do than before he started. Still, his heart's in the right place. Talking of pets, I'm afraid Rhymes is a little down in the dumps at the moment."

"Oh dear. What's the matter with him?"

"It's that girlfriend of his. She's finished with him."

"Oh no. Poor Rhymes. I'll pop up there and see if I can cheer him up."

In the spare bedroom, Barry was dashing around like someone possessed, supposedly tidying the room. Meanwhile, Rhymes was standing quietly in the corner with his head bowed.

"Hey there, Rhymes. How are you?"

"Hello, Jill. I'm okay. I suppose."

"Aunt Lucy told me what happened with Poesy. I'm really sorry."

"She left me for someone else. She said I was boring and that my poetry was awful."

"That was a horrible thing for her to say. Take no notice. I think your poetry is really good. Is there anything I can do to cheer you up?"

"Not really. Unless—err—well, there is one thing, actually."

"Go on. What is it?"

"There's a book I've been wanting to read for a long time now, but I've never been able to find it."

"If you tell me what it is, I'll see if I can track it down for you."

"Thanks, Jill. That's very kind. It's called Thoughts From The Shell, and it's by S. Lowe Walker."

"Okay. I can't make any promises, but I'll see what I can do."

I was just about to leave the room when one of the small ornaments, which Aunt Lucy kept on the shelf above the bed, crashed to the floor and broke. Barry must have knocked it off with his tail.

"Don't worry, Jill," he said. "I'll sweep it up. Everything will be fine."

"Okay, but be careful, and don't cut your paws."

"Did I hear something break up there?" Aunt Lucy said.

"Yes. I'm afraid Barry knocked one of your ornaments off the shelf."

"Don't worry about it. I only keep the ornaments I don't like in there."

"I gave you one of those for your birthday."

"Oh? I—err—I didn't—err—"

"Just joking."

"Oh, right." She gave a sigh of relief. "By the way, have you seen the twins today?"

"No, I haven't. Why?"

"I got the distinct impression that they're planning something big to do with Cuppy C."

"What kind of thing?"

"I don't know. I just happened to overhear them talking, but when I asked them what they were up to, they said it was nothing for me to concern myself with. But you know what they're like with their madcap schemes."

"I certainly do."

"Do you think you could try to find out what's going on, and if it's something stupid, put a stop to it?"

"I'll try, but you know what they're like once they have a bee in their bonnet. I'll pop over there after I leave here. By the way, how is Lester getting on with his new job?"

"He seems to be enjoying it, and I'm slowly getting used to the smell of fish. The money isn't very good, but beggars can't be choosers, so we'll just have to cut our cloth accordingly."

"I know what you mean. Jack and I are struggling money-wise at the moment."

"I'm sorry to hear that, Jill. I'd love to help out, but I can't."

"I wouldn't expect you to. It's got so bad that I've even had to agree to act as Winky's chauffeur, to earn a little extra cash."

"I don't know if it will help or not, but someone popped this leaflet through the letterbox the other day. Something about a way to earn a second income." She handed it to me. "It's not something I'm interested in, but you're welcome to take it with you if you like."

"Thanks. I'll take a proper look at it tonight. Before I go, you couldn't spare another ginger nut, could you?"

"Of course. In fact, why don't you take the packet with you?"

"I couldn't do that."

"I insist."

***

After leaving Aunt Lucy's house, I went straight to Cuppy C, to find out what half-baked plan the twins had come up with this time.

They were both in the shop, but neither of them was behind the counter. Instead, they appeared to be poring over paperwork, at a table at the back of the room.

"Your usual, Jill?" Mindy said.

"Not today, thanks. I've just come from Aunt Lucy's. I had a drink and something to eat there. I want a quick word with the twins. I wasn't sure if they'd be in today or not."

"Yeah, their little ones are upstairs with Jemima."

"Okay, I'd better go and see what they're up to this time."

I walked over to the table, pulled up a chair and sat down. As soon as I did, Pearl grabbed the paperwork and turned it over.

"Okay, you two. What are you up to now?"

"Nothing." Amber shrugged.

"We were just taking our break," Pearl said.

"Why so secretive with the paperwork, then? Can I have a look?" I reached out for it.

"No, you can't." Pearl slapped my hand away.

"I know you two are up to something. So does Aunt Lucy. You might as well tell me because I'm going to find out sooner or later."

"Okay," Amber said. "If you must know, we've decided to close the cake shop."

I was flabbergasted. "You're going to close down

Cuppy C?"

"No, of course not." She rolled her eyes. "We're not closing the tea room. Just the cake shop."

"But why?"

"It simply isn't paying its way anymore."

"Are you going to expand the tea room into there?"

"No. The whole point of the exercise is to reduce the overheads. These were originally two separate units before we took them on. We've spoken to the landlord, and he's agreed that we can release one of the units."

"What will happen to the staff who work in there?"

"There's only a couple of part-timers. If they want to stay on, we'll move them into the tea room."

"I assume you've run all the figures for this."

"Of course we have, and we've talked it through with our accountant. This is the only sensible way forward. The tea room is profitable, but at the moment, it's having to subsidise the cake shop. Once we've closed it, we'll be much better off."

"Fair enough. That makes sense, I suppose. While we're on the subject of tea rooms, you'll never guess where I was the other day."

"Did you go back to the waxwork museum?" Amber suggested. "To admire your sculpture?"

"I most certainly did not. I was actually in the other Candlefield with Martin."

"What *other* Candlefield?" Pearl looked confused. "I wasn't aware there was more than one."

"Neither was I, but it turns out there is. That's where Martin has been all these years. While I was there, we paid a visit to a tea room, just like this one. It's called Bunny B."

The twins looked at one another, then Amber said, "That's a stupid name."

"Yeah." Pearl nodded. "It doesn't work."

"For once, I agree with you. It makes me think of a rabbit and a bumblebee. And you'll never believe this, but it's run by twins."

"Are they like us?" Amber said.

"They're actually guys called Rocky and Stone, and they squabble just like you two."

"We never squabble," Amber objected.

"What are their cakes like?" Pearl asked.

"They're very nice, but obviously not as good as yours."

Just then, I happened to spot a poster on the noticeboard. It was for Candlefield Wax Museum, and it was advertising their new exhibits.

"Why have you got that thing up there?"

"To make sure all of our customers know about your waxwork. Everyone's really keen to see it."

"I don't want anyone to see it. It's horrible, and it looks nothing like me."

"They've definitely captured your nose," Pearl said.

"Why does everyone keep saying that? That stupid sculpture isn't even the same height as me. In fact, I'm going to go over there right now, to demand that they take it off display."

"Spoilsport." Pearl grinned.

***

The woman behind reception at the waxworks wasn't the same one I'd seen on my previous visit.

"Welcome to Candlefield Wax Museum. How can I help

you?"

"I'd like to see Max Kirk, please."

"I'm sorry, but Max is away on holiday for another week, I believe."

"In that case, I'd like to speak to someone else. My name is Jill Maxwell."

"I thought I recognised you. I was looking at the new exhibits earlier."

"But that thing looks nothing like—never mind—I want to speak to someone about having that sculpture taken off display immediately."

"I'm very sorry, Mrs Maxwell, but the only person who can authorise its removal is Max Kirk. I'm afraid you'll have to wait until he's back from holiday."

"Great."

There was no way I was going to wait for Max Kirk to get back, so I made my way to the new exhibits area. It was much quieter there than on my previous visit. The initial interest had obviously died down a little.

I loitered in the background until there was no one else in the room, then I used the 'shrink' spell on my so-called waxwork. After stuffing it into my pocket, I made a quick exit.

* * *

Back at the office, Mrs V was still stressing out about her yarn.

"Sorry to bother you, Mrs V, but do we have any paperclips? I seem to be all out."

"I only put some in your drawer a few days ago."

"That's what I thought, but I can't find any in there

now."

"I'll order some more."

"Thanks."

Winky was sitting on my desk.

"Get off there."

"Not before I give you this." He handed me a sheet of paper.

"What is it?"

"It's a bill for the repair of my phone's screen. It broke when you threw it out of the window. The man in the shop said it was lucky that it didn't do more damage."

"I'm not paying that." I thrust the invoice back into his paw.

Before he could argue, the door flew open, and Kathy came charging into the office. She was red in the face and clearly raging about something. Winky took one look at her, jumped off the desk and hid under the sofa.

"Kathy? What's wrong?"

"*What's wrong*? I'll tell you what's wrong. That husband of mine, that's what's wrong."

"What's Peter done?"

"He's only gone and told Mikey that he'll take him go-karting."

"But I thought you said he wouldn't be allowed to go until he was older."

"I did. That's what Pete and I agreed, but then while they were fishing, Mikey managed to persuade Pete to change his mind."

"Can't *you* put your foot down and say he can't go?"

"And look like the Wicked Witch of The West? It's too late for that now, but if anything happens to Mikey, Pete will be sorry."

"Would you like a drink or something?"

"No, thanks. I can't stop. I had a couple of errands to run on the high street, so I thought I'd pop in, and let off some steam. Plus, I wanted to ask you about Martin. I thought everything was going alright when he came over to our house, until he rushed off. I assume I must have done something to upset him."

"Don't be silly. Of course you didn't. He really enjoyed meeting you."

"So how come he rushed off like that? Did he tell you why he'd done it?"

"Just that it was something to do with work, but everything's fine, honestly."

"Will I get to see him again soon?"

"I'm sure you will. Especially now that he and I are getting along better."

"Are you? It felt like there was some tension between the two of you."

"There was, but we've had a long talk since then, and we've cleared the air."

"That's good to hear. Do you have any idea what his plans are? Does he intend to live up here permanently?"

"I'm not sure, but I think he probably will."

Chapter 3

I'd been feeling a little under the weather ever since I'd got up that morning, so after Kathy left, I decided to call it a day. It felt as though I might be coming down with a cold, and I couldn't stop my nose running. I pulled a tissue out of my pocket, and as I did, the shrunken waxwork figure dropped onto the floor.

Before I could react, Winky ran across the room and picked it up.

"You bought me a replica of your waxwork. Thank you, Jill."

"No, hang on."

"I shall give this pride of place in the office."

"Give that to me." I snatched it from him.

"Hey, you can't take it back. You gave me that as a present."

"No, I didn't. Now get out of my way." I stuffed it into my pocket and went through to the outer office.

"I'm going home, Mrs V. I'm feeling a bit under the weather."

"Alright, dear. I hope you feel better soon."

***

As I approached the outskirts of Smallwash, I spotted a familiar white van parked at the side of the road. It was my good friend, Harry Hart, the window cleaner. Just the man I wanted to talk to about the seventy-five pounds bill I'd had to pay to get the kitchen window replaced.

I knocked on the driver's side window.

"You made me jump, Mrs Maxwell. What can I do for

you?"

"You can start by repaying the seventy-five pounds I had to spend to replace the window that stupid robot of yours broke."

"I don't know what you're talking about."

"Don't come the innocent with me, Harry. It isn't going to wash. Robbie broke my kitchen window, as well you know."

"You must be mistaken. Robbie is a precision tool."

"The only *tool* around here is you."

"It could have been a burglar."

"This wasn't a burglary. Robbie broke the window, and I expect you to reimburse me for the cost of the replacement."

"I'm sorry, Mrs Maxwell, but there's no way that Robbie—"

He was interrupted by the sound of breaking glass, coming from the house in front of which Harry was parked. His face fell.

"What could that be, I wonder?" I said. "Shall we take a look?"

He followed me up the driveway and around the back of the house.

There was Robbie with one of his metal 'hands' sticking through the broken windowpane. Inside the house, a woman who looked none too pleased, began to yell at Harry, "I thought you said this robot of yours was cutting edge technology? Look what it's done to my window."

By the time I got back to my car, Harry had refunded my seventy-five pounds and compensated the woman.

"By the way, Harry," I shouted as he loaded Robbie into the back of his van. "I'm sure I don't need to tell you that we won't be requiring your services again."

***

Jack pulled onto the driveway just ahead of me. As we got out of our cars, the Livelys were coming out of their house.

"Hi, Kit," Jack shouted. "Hi, Britt."

Why did Jack insist on being so sociable? We could have sneaked into the house before they spotted us.

"Hi there." Kit waved back.

I felt awful and all I wanted to do was go inside and put my feet up, but Jack went over to talk to them, so I had no option but to join him.

"How are you both?" Jack said. "You look a little down in the dumps."

"To tell you the truth, we've been doing a lot of soul searching these last few days," Kit said.

"What about?"

"It all stems from what happened in the marathon. I suppose we've both been guilty of thinking that we'd be able to maintain our high levels of fitness forever. But, as Jill rightly pointed out, time catches up with everyone eventually."

"Don't be silly." Jack laughed. "You two are still in the prime of your life."

"Not if our marathon performance is anything to go by." Britt sighed. "You saw the times we posted."

"Everyone has an off-day."

"That's true, but we both work in the fitness industry, and no one will want to hire a personal trainer who gets out of breath walking up a flight of stairs."

"Now you're exaggerating," Jack said. "You both look perfectly fit to me. One bad race shouldn't cause you to have doubts like this."

"We haven't made any firm decisions yet. We'll have to see how we feel in a few weeks' time," Kit said. "Anyway, we must get going. We're meeting friends for dinner."

After they'd left, Jack gave me a look.

"What? Why are you looking at me like that?"

"You heard what Kit just said. They're thinking of changing their careers, and all because of what happened in the marathon."

"So?" I shrugged.

"*So*, the only reason their times were so bad is because you used magic to slow them down."

"Yes, but there was a good reason for that. If you remember, they were going to fleece us on the sponsorship."

"I still think you should say something to them, Jill."

"And what exactly would you have me say? That the only reason they performed so poorly is because I used magic to slow them down? Is that really what you want me to do?"

"No, obviously you can't say that."

"What then?"

"I don't know. It just seems so unfair."

"You're too soft, Jack. They'd gladly have taken our money under false pretences. Anyway, never mind all that. I'm hungry. Whose turn is it to make dinner?"

"It's yours. I made steak and kidney pie last night."

"Did you? Oh yes." I sighed. "To tell you the truth, I'm really in the mood for pizza."

"Fair enough. I'd be up for that." He took out his phone.

"I'll order it now. What do you want?"

"My usual, but with anchovies."

He looked at me like I'd grown a second head. "You *hate* anchovies."

"Well, I fancy some today."

***

"That was delicious." I wiped a crumb from my lips.

Jack stared at my plate. "You've left half of it."

"I ate all the anchovies."

"I think you must be sickening for something."

"I felt a bit queasy earlier, but I feel much better now that I have some food inside me. By the way, I went to Cuppy C today. The twins have decided to close down the cake shop."

"They're closing Cuppy C?"

"No, that's what I thought at first, but they're only closing the cake shop part of the business. The tea room will carry on as usual. Apparently, the cake shop hasn't been paying its way for some time now, so they've talked to the landlord who has agreed that they can hand back that part of the unit."

"I assume they know what they're doing."

"That's quite an assumption, but they insist they've been through all the figures, and they've spoken to their accountant."

"I guess we're not the only ones who are feeling the pinch at the moment."

"That reminds me." I grabbed my bag and took out the leaflet. "Aunt Lucy gave me this."

"What is it?"

I read it out loud, *"Need extra cash? An ideal second income can be had by providing safe accommodation to ruby fairies during their hibernation season. Very little work involved."*

"Ruby fairies? What are they?"

"I'm not sure, but if they're anything like starlight fairies, they'll be tiny little things."

"The leaflet talks about fostering them. What would that entail?"

"I have no idea, but if they're hibernating, how difficult can it be? We'd probably just have to provide them with a warm safe place to sleep."

"Like where?"

"Jeez, Jack, I don't know. The airing cupboard, maybe."

"Will they let you bring them to the human world?"

"I'm not sure. Maybe not, but it's worth checking out. We could certainly do with the cash. I'll give them a call tomorrow. It's not like we have anything to lose."

"Okay. Go for it."

"By the way, it sounds like Peter's in big trouble."

"Why? What's he done now?"

"Kathy came to see me today, and she was spitting feathers. Apparently, Peter took Mikey fishing the other day and while they were there, Mikey managed to persuade his dad to let him go go-karting."

"Really? That'll be brilliant."

"Kathy doesn't think so. Apparently, she and Peter had discussed it beforehand, and they'd agreed that Mikey wouldn't be allowed to do it until he was older, but then Peter caved in. Kathy was not impressed."

"Do you think I'll be able to go with them? I've always fancied go-karting."

"Don't you have enough hobbies already? What with your ten-pin bowling and your train set? I thought we were trying to cut back on costs."

"Sorry, you're right." He sighed. "Go-karting would be a blast, though."

I'd just started to load the dishwasher when there was a knock at the door.

"I'll get it." Jack jumped up.

Moments later, I heard several excited voices in the hallway. I should have known better, but curiosity got the better of me, so I went to find out who it was.

I shouldn't have bothered.

Tony and Clare, our next-door neighbours, were there. So too was Mr Hosey. All four of them were clearly excited about something. I wanted no part of it, so I turned to go back to the kitchen.

I wasn't quick enough, though.

"Hi, Jill," Mr Hosey said.

"Hi," Tony and Clare chorused.

"Hello, you three."

"Would you like to come with us, too?" Clare said.

The answer was almost definitely 'no', but to be polite, I felt I should at least show some interest. "Come with you where?"

"We were just telling Jack that it's TrainCon this Sunday."

"They've asked if I'd like to go with them." Jack sounded as excited as a young kid on Christmas morning. "I've said I'll go. Why don't you come too?"

"With you, Tony and Clare, *and* Mr Hosey?"

"Yeah."

"And dress up as a train?"

"That's right."

"Err, let me think about that." I paused, strictly for effect. "No, thanks. I'm going to give that one a miss."

"But it could be fun. You don't have to dress up as a train; you could be a signal box."

"A signal box? Cool."

"Do you fancy it, then?"

"No. I'm sure you four (saddos) will enjoy it, but I'm going to pass."

***

I was in the middle of a lovely dream, which for some crazy reason featured fluffy bunny rabbits and cocktails, when something woke me up.

I checked the clock at the side of the bed to find it was two-thirty in the morning. Had I really heard something, or had I just imagined it? I rolled over and was about to try and go back to sleep when I heard the sound again: Someone was knocking at the door.

Who could that be at this hour?

I nudged Jack. "There's someone at the door."

"Cabbages, please," he said, without opening his eyes.

"Jack, did you hear me?"

Clearly, he hadn't because he began to snore.

Great! "I'll go and check who it is then, shall I?" I threw on my dressing gown, hurried downstairs and put on the hall light.

"Who's there?" I shouted through the door.

All I could hear was a kind of groaning sound, so I tried again, "Who's out there?"

The groaning continued, and then whoever it was pounded on the door again.

"I'm going to open the door, but if you try any funny business, you'll be sorry."

They would too. I was just in the mood to turn someone into a cockroach.

I opened the door to find a zombie standing there. I was just about to blast it with the 'thunderbolt' spell when it spoke. That in itself took me by surprise because, although I'd encountered many zombies, I'd never heard one speak before. I had no idea that they could.

"It's me, Jill," the zombie said.

"Sorry, do I know you?"

"It's me, Ike Cann."

"Ike, what happened to you? Did you die?"

"No, I'm still alive."

"Are you sure?"

"Yeah. I know I look like a zombie, but I'm not really."

"You're doing a very good impression of one."

"I know. That's the problem."

"What happened?"

"I fell out with my next-door neighbour who's a wizard. To cut a long story short, he was the one who did this to me. He made me look like a zombie, knowing full well what could happen. If anyone from Z-Watch spots me, they'll destroy me. I didn't know what to do or where to go, but then I remembered that you're a witch. I thought maybe you'd be able to help."

"How do I know it's actually you, Ike? You could be anyone."

He thought about it for a moment. "I could tell you your passphrase. Would that persuade you?"

"I suppose so."

"It's 'crazy just got crazier'."

"Okay, I believe you. You'd better come inside before someone sees you. Try not to drop any body parts on the floor." He shuffled into the house. "Go and take a seat in the kitchen while I check my spell book, to see if I can find a spell that can sort this out."

Once he was in the kitchen, I went through to the lounge, and began to flick through my book of advanced spells. I'd only got a few pages in when I heard a yell. I rushed into the hall where I found Jack, looking as white as a sheet.

"There's a zombie in the kitchen."

"It's okay. That's not a zombie."

"Yes, it is."

"I know it looks like one, but it's actually Ike Cann from Z-Watch. A wizard cast a spell to make him look like that."

"Are you sure?"

"I'm positive. Ike just quoted my Z-Watch passphrase. Only he would be able to do that. Why don't you go back to bed while I sort this out?"

"Are you sure you'll be okay?"

"I'll be fine. Off you go."

Reluctantly, he made his way upstairs, and I went back to studying the book of spells.

Thirty minutes later, I joined Ike at the kitchen table.

"I've been all the way through my spell book, and I can't see anything that is going to sort this out."

"What am I going to do, Jill?"

"You'll have to stay in our spare bedroom tonight. I'll go and talk to Grandma tomorrow. If anyone will know what to do, she will."

Chapter 4

The next morning, at breakfast, Jack could hardly keep his eyes open.

"Are you all right?" I said.

"Not really. I couldn't get back to sleep last night. Not with that *thing* in the next room."

"I told you that Ike isn't a real zombie. He just looks like one."

"That doesn't really help. Even if I'd managed to get to sleep, I would only have had nightmares. How long is he going to be staying with us?"

"Hopefully, he'll be gone before the day is out. That's if I can get hold of Grandma, and she can tell me how to turn him back to his old self."

Those words were no sooner out of my mouth than my phone rang; it was Grandma. How did she do that?

"Grandma, how did you know that I was going—"

"I need you over here straight away, Jill. It's a matter of life and death."

"What's wrong?"

"Just get over here. I'm at my house. Make it quick." With that, she put the phone down.

"I've been summoned by Grandma."

"What does she want?"

"No idea. She didn't say."

"You can't leave me here alone with that thing upstairs."

"You have nothing to fear from Ike. He's harmless." I laughed. "He'll be legless too if they drop off."

"This isn't a laughing matter, Jill."

"Sorry, but I can't do anything until I've spoken to

Grandma. She's the only one who might be able to sort this zombie thing out."

"Will you at least get him some breakfast before you go?"

"I don't have time. You'll have to do that."

"What do you think he'll want to eat?"

"I don't know. Human brains, maybe?"

"That's not funny."

"Just give him some Weetabix."

"I haven't heard him moving around yet, have you?"

"No. I'm surprised he isn't awake because it can't have been easy sleeping on the floor with your train set in there."

"I hope he hasn't broken anything." Jack frowned.

"I'd better get going. When Ike wakes up tell him I'm trying to sort something out for him, will you?"

"If I'm here. With a bit of luck, I'll be gone before he comes down."

***

I magicked myself over to Grandma's house. There was no sign of her downstairs.

"Grandma," I shouted. "Where are you?"

"Up here in the bedroom."

"Are you poorly?" I hurried upstairs.

"Not exactly."

"What's the—" I stopped mid-sentence because I'd spotted the wart on the end of her nose; it was turning from red to amber and then to green.

"What are you staring at?" she snapped.

"Err, nothing."

"Now you see why I wanted you to come straight over." She poked the wart with her finger. "It started doing this an hour ago."

"What's wrong with it?"

"If I knew that, I wouldn't have called you, would I?"

"Shall I call the doctor?"

"That won't do any good. I need you to find a potion to sort it out."

"I'm not too hot on potions."

"I know that. I wasn't asking you to come up with one. I just need you to find Rhonda Rules."

"Who's she?"

"Rhonda is the last word in potions. If anyone will know how to sort this out, she will. I want you to go and find her, explain my predicament, and ask her to come up with a suitable potion."

I took out my phone and pointed it at Grandma.

"Hey, what are you doing?"

"I thought I'd take a video of the wart. It'll be easier than trying to explain it to Rhonda."

"Okay, but just make sure you destroy it once she's seen it."

"Will do. Smile for the camera."

She scowled. "That's enough. Rhonda will get the idea."

"While I'm here, Grandma, can I ask you about a zombie-related problem?"

"No, you can't. Not until my nose is restored to its former glory. Go and find Rhonda."

"Do you have any idea where I should look for her?"

"You could try asking for her at the Three Merry Turkeys. They'll probably know where she is."

"Where's that?"

"It's a public house in the marketplace, between the chiropodist and the artichoke shop."

"Okay, I'll pop over there now."

I knew where the chiropodist was because I'd had to go there once before to pick up some bunion ointment for Grandma. The sign outside the public house next door was quite distinctive: A picture of three turkeys, who as the name suggested, looked very merry indeed.

I've been in some dives in my time, but I can honestly say that the Three Merry Turkeys was the worst pub I'd ever had the misfortune to set foot in. The place was filthy and smelled awful. As I walked over to the bar, my shoes kept sticking to the floor. There were precious few windows, and those that there were, were covered in grime, and allowed practically no light into the place. On reflection, that was probably a blessing because I could already see way more than I wanted to.

It was still early morning, but there were already a few customers in there. As far as I could make out, I was the only female present. Behind the bar, a wizard who had several days' stubble, and a cigarette sticking out of the corner of his mouth, eyed me suspiciously.

"What can I get for you, Missy?" As he spoke, ash dropped onto the counter.

"I'm not here for a drink. I was told that I might find Rhonda Rules in here."

"Rhonda?" He wiped his forearm across his nose. "Oh yeah. She's always here."

"Where will I find her?"

"Upstairs in one of the bedrooms; she's sleeping off last night's session. I wouldn't disturb her if you know what's good for you."

"This is urgent. I need to speak to her straight away."

"On your head be it, then."

"Which room is she in?"

"Your guess is as good as mine. There are only six of them up there, so it shouldn't take you long to find her."

Once I was upstairs, I found myself in a dingy corridor, which was illuminated by a single low-powered light.

The first door I tried was locked. The second one opened to reveal a big fat wizard, fast asleep on the floor; he was snoring his head off. The third room was unlocked, but there was no one inside. In the fourth, I struck gold. Fast asleep, on top of the bed covers, and still fully dressed, was a witch.

As I got closer, I could see that she'd dribbled all over the pillow. It was not a pretty sight.

"Rhonda?" There was no response. "Rhonda, is that you?" I gave her a little shake, but there was still no response. "Rhonda, wake up," I shouted.

She sat up with a start. "What's going on? Where am I? Is there a fire?"

"No, it's okay. I'm sorry to wake you."

"What time is it?"

"Just turned nine."

"At night?"

"No, in the morning."

"What?" She slumped back onto the pillow. "Why are you waking me up at this time of day?"

"Please, Rhonda, this is very urgent. I've been sent here by Mirabel Millbright."

"Mirabel?" She opened her eyes again and sat up. "What does she want?"

I took out my phone and showed her the video of Grandma's nose.

Rhonda laughed. "Ouch! That hurts." She rubbed her forehead.

"Can you help? Do you know what could have caused this?"

"Oh yes. I've seen that a few times before."

"What is it?"

"TLN syndrome."

"*TLN*? What's that?"

"It stands for Traffic Light Nose syndrome."

"Do you have a potion that will sort it out?"

"Not on me, but I do know of one. Now, let me think. Oh yes. Rat hair and thistle. That's it."

"Rat hair and thistle? Are you sure?"

"Positive."

"Where would I find it?"

"Try Abigail's Apothecary. Over on the other side of the market, you'll find a narrow alleyway. It's down there." She lay back down. "I really must go back to sleep now because my head's thumping."

It was a great relief to get outside into the fresh air.

I followed Rhonda's directions to Abigail's Apothecary. The tiny shop was empty except for the young witch behind the counter.

"Hi, are you Abigail?"

"No, I'm Patricia. Abigail died several years ago."

"I was advised to come here by Rhonda Rules. She told me that I need rat hair and thistle potion."

"Are you absolutely sure that's what she said?"

"Definitely."

"Okay. It's just that I don't get much demand for that. Just give me a minute, would you?"

She slid the ladder from one side of the room to the other, then climbed high enough to allow her to reach the top shelf from which she took a small jar. Back at the counter, she passed it to me.

"That will be fifteen pounds and ninety-seven pence, please."

I handed over the cash. Hopefully, Grandma would reimburse me later.

With the jar tucked safely in my pocket, I magicked myself back to Grandma's house.

"What took you so long?" she snapped.

"I was as quick as I could be. Rhonda Rules was rather the worse for wear; it took me a while to wake her."

"Did you get what I asked for?"

"Yes." I handed her the jar.

"Rat hair and thistle? Are you sure this is what she recommended?"

"Positive. Rhonda said that will do the trick."

"Okay, you can go now."

"Just a minute, Grandma."

"Don't worry. I'll give you the money later."

"It's not that. I wanted to ask you about the zombie."

"What about it?"

"A friend of mine has been turned into a zombie-lookalike, and I need to know how to reverse the spell."

"How am I supposed to know how to do it?"

"You know most spells."

"That's true, but I don't know this one. Have you checked your spell book?"

"Of course I have. That's the first thing I did."

"Are you sure your book is up-to-date?"

"What do you mean?"

"Don't tell me that you've never updated your spell book."

"I didn't realise you could. How would I do that?"

"Look at the very last page in the book. There's a full explanation there. Now, leave me alone so I can focus on this wart, would you?"

***

I magicked myself back to the house, so I could pick up the car and check on Ike, to see how he was doing. I found him in the kitchen.

"I hope you don't mind me helping myself to corn flakes," he said.

"Of course not. Our house is your house while you're here."

I noticed that one of his fingers had dropped off onto the kitchen table, but I thought it best not to mention it.

"Did you have any luck finding a way to reverse the spell, Jill?" he asked, eagerly.

"I'm afraid not. I've spoken to Grandma, but she doesn't know how to do it. She suggested that if I update my spell book, there might be something in the newer edition. I don't have time to do it now because I need to get to work, but I'll do it as soon as I get home tonight. Will you be okay to stay here until then?"

"I suppose so."

"Don't go outside, Ike, whatever you do."

"Don't worry. I won't. It's much too dangerous. Is it

okay if I watch TV?"

"Yes, but if anyone comes to the door, don't answer it. And stay well away from the windows. I don't want you to scare the neighbours. No offence."

"None taken."

***

After I'd parked in Washbridge, I took a walk down to Coffee Games. I was going to need some caffeine to get me through the day.

Inside, I found people lying blindfolded on the floor; they all seemed to be holding rolled-up newspapers and magazines. By now, I shouldn't have been surprised by anything that happened in that shop, but this was particularly weird even by their standards.

Piers was behind the counter.

"What's today's game, Piers?"

"Apparently, it's called 'Are you there, Moriarty?'"

"How does it work?"

"To tell you the truth, Jill, I don't really know. It's all a bit stupid if you ask me. Basically, they have to try to hit each other with newspapers, I think. And they keep shouting out, 'Are you there, Moriarty?'"

Right on cue, one of the people lying on the floor closest to me, shouted those exact words, and tried to hit the man next to him, with a rolled-up newspaper.

"I think you'd better make that coffee to-go, please. I don't think I can handle this nonsense."

"Would you like anything to eat with it, Jill?"

"No, thanks. Not this morning. Just the coffee, please."

As I walked up the high street, Betty Longbottom came out of her shop and called me over.

"Good morning, Jill." She wasn't speaking in her fake posh voice, so I assumed that the TV crew weren't anywhere around.

"Morning, Betty. You're looking particularly pleased with life."

"I am, and it's all thanks to the TV show. It's the best thing that's ever happened to me. Since it went on air, the marine centre and shop have been buzzing. Takings are up almost five hundred percent. If it carries on like this, I'll have to give serious consideration to opening another shop, maybe in West Chipping."

"That's great. I'm really pleased for you, but I must get going. I have a busy day ahead."

"Okay, catch you later."

It was now official: I was a complete idiot.

Here I was, struggling for cash, and desperate to attract more clients, and yet I'd turned down the chance to be in a reality TV show. Betty had taken full advantage of it, and now her businesses were going from strength to strength as a result. When would I ever learn?

Chapter 5

When I arrived at the office, Mrs V was frantic.

"Whatever's wrong, Mrs V?"

"They've been at it again."

"*Who's* been at *what* again?"

"Those bugs, or whatever it is that's been eating my yarn. The linen basket was still half full when I went home last night, but just look at it now: It's almost all gone, and what's left is in shreds." She was clearly upset.

I peered into the basket: it was a real mess. Something had decimated what was left of her yarn.

"Have you actually seen any of the bugs yet, Mrs V?"

"No. That's the really frustrating part. I've just spent the last fifteen minutes going through what's left of the yarn, but there's no sign of them. I don't understand what's happening, Jill. How can they disappear like that?"

"I have no idea. Maybe if you bought a new linen basket, that would do the trick."

"If I thought it would do any good, I would, but who's to say that those little blighters won't just do the same thing again? I'm never going to get those jumpers knitted in time."

I felt really sorry for Mrs V, but there was nothing I could do, other than to offer my sympathy.

As soon as I walked into my office, Winky scurried under the sofa.

"What are you up to?" I said.

"Me? Nothing."

"You're definitely up to something. Why else would you have dived under there?"

"I don't know what you're talking about. Nothing to see

here."

"Very convincing, I don't think. Get out here."

He continued to fiddle with something for a minute or so, and then emerged, looking all innocent-like.

"What were you doing under there, Winky?"

"I've already told you. I wasn't doing anything."

"Whatever it is you're up to, it had better not cost me any money."

I didn't trust that cat as far as I could throw him, but I couldn't waste any more time on him because I needed to do some research on the Kramer case.

I started by going online and searching The Bugles' archives where I found several articles related to the murder of Alison Reed. I didn't learn a whole lot from them that I didn't already know, but I did find the name of the detective who'd been in charge of the case at the time: Walter Staniforth. A separate search on his name revealed that he'd retired four years ago. The 'human interest' article said that he was hoping to have more time for his hobby of fishing, and that he had just moved to a new house in the village of Middle Tweaking.

On the basis of that information, I made a phone call to Myrtle Turtle.

"Turtle speaking."

"Myrtle, it's Jill Maxwell."

"Hello, Jill. I was reading the paper the other day, and something in there put me in mind of you."

"Really? Was it an article on famous private investigators?"

"Actually, it was an item about a shortage of custard creams."

"Right. Look, the reason I've called is that I was

wondering if you might know a gentleman by the name of Walter Staniforth? He was a detective in Washbridge before he retired to live in Middle Tweaking."

"Yes, I know Walter. He's been living in the village for a couple of years now, I believe. Why do you ask?"

"I'm currently working on a murder case that dates back five years; a young woman was poisoned. My clients' son was convicted of her murder and is currently serving time. His parents are convinced of his innocence, and they've asked me to look into the case. I've just discovered that Mr Staniforth was the officer in charge of the investigation at the time, and I'm hoping to speak to him. Can you tell me anything about him?"

"Not much really, Jill. To tell you the truth, he's a bit of a funny fellow who hasn't really integrated into village life. I get on with him okay, but we only normally exchange a 'good morning' or a 'good evening'. We did bond a little over our mutual dislike of tourists who insist on parking on the village green, but other than that, I've not really had any meaningful conversations with him. From what other people have told me, they find him rather standoffish, but I think it's just that he likes to keep himself to himself."

"Is there any chance you could introduce me to him? He might be more receptive to my questions that way, rather than if I just turned up on his doorstep."

"I can certainly try, but I'm not promising anything."

"That's all I can ask."

"I'll make it my business to bump into him as soon as I can, and I'll let you know how I get on."

"Thanks Myrtle. I really appreciate it."

***

I wanted to find out more about the ruby fairy foster scheme, so I called the number on the leaflet.

"Good morning. Ruby fairy foster line, Jessica Diamond speaking, how can I help you today?"

"Hi. My name is Jill Maxwell. I have one of your leaflets in front of me, and I have a few questions."

"Yes, madam. What would you like to know?"

"I was considering participating in the scheme, but I live in the human world and wondered if that might rule me out?"

"Absolutely not. Quite a few sups who live in the human world have fostered ruby fairies. Provided that your husband or partner is also a sup, which I assume he is, then there's no problem."

"Err—right, okay. Could you tell me a little more about what's involved?"

"It's quite simple, really. Ruby fairies hibernate for three months out of the year, and while they're hibernating, they can be susceptible to the elements, and also to a number of rather unpleasant predators. That's why the foster scheme was created. By finding them safe homes where they can hibernate, we can ensure they're safe from those threats."

"I see, and what would I actually have to do?"

"There's not a lot to do, madam. You simply provide them with a comfortable warm place to sleep for three months."

"Do I have to feed them or anything like that?"

"No, they don't need food or drink during the hibernation period. Just a warm place where they can sleep. After three months, when they wake up, they'll return to their homes in Candlefield and carry on with their lives."

"I see. That all sounds very straightforward. Would it be appropriate of me to ask what the payment is?"

"Of course. It's based on the number of ruby fairies fostered. It's ten pounds PFPD."

"PFPD?"

"Per fairy per day. That equates to just over nine hundred pounds for the hibernation period for a single fairy."

"And how many fairies do people normally foster at a time?"

"The average is two, and five is the upper limit."

"I see. Well, if it's okay with you, I think we'd like to go for the maximum number. In for a penny, in for a pound."

"Certainly, madam. Would you like me to put you down for five?"

"Yes, please. Where would I have to collect them from?"

"That won't be necessary. They'll be delivered to your place of residence, and collected from there at the end of the hibernation period."

"Fantastic. And when would all of this take place?"

"If you sign up today, they'll be delivered to you next Monday."

"Brilliant. Let's do it."

"Okay, madam. If you give me your details, I can get the ball rolling."

"What was that all about?" Winky asked when I came off the phone.

"None of your business."

"Come on. Tell me."

"If you must know. Jack and I have decided to provide a home for some ruby fairies while they hibernate."

"And why would you want to do that?"

"It seems like a public-spirited thing to do."

"Nothing to do with the money, then?"

"That doesn't come into it."

"Pull the other one. I could see the pound signs in your eyes."

"Rubbish."

***

When I stepped out of my office building, the temperature seemed to have dropped several degrees; it was easily the coldest day of the year so far. Which was why I found it so surprising that there was an ice cream van parked at the side of the road, near to the car park. What kind of idiot would try to sell ice cream in this weather?

As I walked past, I spotted a familiar face in the van. Two familiar faces, in fact: It was Daze and Blaze.

"What are you two doing here?"

"Shush!" Daze put a finger to her lips. "You mustn't blow our cover."

"Sorry. Who are you after this time?"

"Ice nymphs," Blaze said. "I hate those guys with a passion."

"I've never heard of ice nymphs. I've had some dealings with wood nymphs recently, and they've caused me nothing but grief."

"Wood nymphs are a pushover." Daze rolled her eyes.

"Just wait until you come across ice nymphs. They're really sinister creatures."

I glanced up at the large ice cream cone on top of the van. "Far be it from me to criticise, Daze, but this isn't the best undercover operation you've ever mounted. It's freezing cold today. Don't you think people will find it a little suspicious when they see an ice cream van parked at the side of the road?"

"I'm sure they will." She sighed. "It's RR admin who are at fault. They're a useless bunch. We put in a request for a burger van and this is what they gave us. I had a right go at them this morning, but they said the soonest they could get us a burger van would be a couple of days, so we're stuck with this thing. We stand out like a sore thumb."

"What exactly have the ice nymphs been doing?"

"Can't you tell?"

"I don't know what you mean."

"Surely you must have noticed the sudden drop in temperature?"

"I assumed it was a cold snap."

"It's been exceptionally mild recently, and the forecast was that it would continue like that for the next few weeks, but the ice nymphs put paid to that."

"Why would they do that?"

"They're called ice nymphs for a reason. They can't survive for long in the warm."

"Why don't they go to the North Pole, then?"

"I wish they would, but they like the city life, particularly Washbridge. That's why they've caused the temperature to drop so dramatically."

"That's a horrible thing to do. Are you saying the

temperature is likely to stay like this until you catch them?"

"If anything, it's going to get worse. That's why it's urgent we track them down."

"Is there anything I can do to help?"

"Not unless you happen to see them."

"What do they look like?"

"You said you're familiar with wood nymphs. The ice nymphs look pretty much the same except they have icicles hanging from their limbs."

"Okay. If I spot them, I'll give you a call."

"Thanks. While you're here, can I interest you in a cornet?"

"Err, no thanks. I'll give it a miss."

***

I was headed for the fast food restaurant where Arnold Kramer had been working at the time of Alison Reed's murder. I'd telephoned ahead and spoken to the manager, a Mr Jordan Coombes, who had said I was welcome to pop in at any time.

When I arrived there, I asked at the counter to speak to the manager. A few minutes later, Jordan, a young man in his twenties, took me through to a small office at the back. He was a good-looking guy with exceptionally small ears.

"Thank you for seeing me, Mr Coombes."

"Call me Jordan. Nobody calls me Mr Coombes. How can I help you? You said on the phone that you were a private investigator."

"That's right. I'm investigating the murder of a young

woman called Alison Reed. She died five years ago after being poisoned by food bought from these premises. Her ex-boyfriend at the time was convicted of her murder. It's his parents who have hired me to look into the case."

"I remember that. It was a terrible business."

"Were you by any chance working here at the time?"

"No, I was still at university then. I've just come through the graduate training scheme. This is my first job; I only took over as manager a few weeks ago. I don't know if you're aware, but the restaurant was forced to close down not long after the tragic incident you're investigating because of the dramatic drop-off in trade caused by the bad publicity. About a year later, the current owner bought the business out of administration, had the building completely revamped, and opened again under a different name."

"I see. I don't suppose any of the people who worked in the previous business work here now, do they?"

"The only person I can think of is Susan Brown. I remember her mentioning to me that she used to work here back then."

"Would it be possible for me to speak to her?"

"I'm afraid not. She's on maternity leave at the moment. In fact, I heard this morning that she had a baby girl yesterday, so she probably won't be able to see you for a while."

"Okay. I'll give it a few days before I try to get in touch with her. In the meantime, can you tell me if the drive-thru is the same now as it was back then?"

"Yes. In fact, that's the only part of the building that is still the same."

"In that case, is it okay if I take a look at it?"

"Of course. Help yourself."

I went back to the car and took it through the drive-thru. I'd only intended to take a look around, but I was tempted by the breakfast menu, and ended up ordering a sausage and egg muffin. After paying at the first window, I collected my food from the second one.

"There you are, madam." The young woman handed me a bag. "One sausage and egg muffin. Have a nice day."

"Thank you very much."

It was a little creepy to think that Alison Reed had collected the food that killed her from that very window. Not creepy enough to stop me devouring the muffin, though.

Chapter 6

Maybe I'd been a little rash when I'd agreed to look for that book for Rhymes; I didn't even know where to start. With little or no expectation, I'd checked Candlefield Pages, and to my utter amazement and delight, I found a section titled 'Rare Tortoise Books'. There was only one entry, but that was one more than I could have hoped for.

The book shop was called Harvey's Booksheller; a name that brought a smile to my face. It was located a couple of miles outside of Candlefield town centre. As it was such a nice day, I magicked myself to the marketplace and walked from there.

Harvey's Booksheller was a tiny establishment. I couldn't even see into the shop because the window was stacked high with all manner of books. It wasn't what you'd call a display; there were just piles upon piles of them blocking the view.

When I walked through the door, a little bell chimed. Once inside, I was confronted by even more piles of books, which stretched all the way to the ceiling, and formed a kind of corridor. I couldn't see the counter, so I simply weaved my way between the walls of books. Eventually, I arrived at a rather dusty counter, behind which, seated on a tall stool, was a tortoise wearing a monocle.

"Good morning, young lady. How can I help you?"

"Are you Harvey, by any chance?"

"I am indeed. Harvey Baskerville at your service."

"You have an awful lot of books in here. Are they all written by tortoises?"

"Not just tortoises. Testudinidae of all types. The number has grown to the point where I'm not sure I have room for anymore. Unless, of course, you're here to take some off my hands?"

"Actually, I'm looking for one book in particular: Thoughts From The Shell by S. Lowe Walker. Have you heard of it?"

"I have indeed. Mr Walker is one of our most respected philosophers."

"Do you happen to have the book, by any chance?"

"I believe I do. Would you be interested in purchasing it?"

"Yes, provided the price is reasonable."

"I would want twenty-five pounds for that particular book. How does that sound?"

"That's fine. I'd like to take it, please."

"Hmm?" He rubbed his chin. "There lies a minor problem."

"I thought you said you had a copy?"

"I do." He looked at the piles of books. "Somewhere. The question is where."

"Don't you catalogue the books?"

"I used to years ago, but I got bored with having to keep updating it. Now, I just put them in piles."

"So, you have the book, but you have no idea where it is?"

"That's right, but I can probably narrow it down to one of those five piles over there because I seem to remember purchasing it within the last two years."

"If I leave it with you, is there any chance you'll be able to find it for me?"

"Yes, of course, but it will take a while, I'm afraid."

"I'll give you my phone number." I handed him my business card. "Would you give me a call when you've found it?"

"Certainly. Is the book for you?"

"Actually, it's for a friend: a tortoise by the name of Rhymes."

"Is he well read?"

"I don't really know. He is a poet, though." Allegedly.

"How very interesting. Has he published anything?"

"As a matter of fact, he has. He published a poetry book recently which won an award."

"How thrilling. If you ask him to let me have a few copies, I'll try to sell them for him. I like to support local authors."

"I'll do that. Thanks, Harvey. And you'll give me a call when you find the book?"

"Rest assured, I'll call you the moment I locate it."

Back at the office, I'd only been at my desk for a few minutes when Mrs V came through the door.

"Jill, I have a gentleman out there who wonders if you have the time to see him. His name is Moriarty."

Moriarty? A likely story. Somebody was trying to take me for the fool. Under normal circumstances, I'd have suspected Grandma, but she was still recovering from traffic light nose syndrome. Who else could it be, I wondered?

"Jill? Can you see him?" Mrs V was still standing there.

"Sorry, yes, would you show the gentleman in, please?"

As soon as he walked through the door, I noticed that he was hobbling. It had to be Martin. Fancied himself as a practical joker, did he? He'd have to get up much earlier in the morning to fool me. I was just about to confront him, but then I thought better of it. I'd play along for a while and then turn the tables on him.

His disguise was well over the top, and truly pathetic. For a start, there clearly was no glass in his spectacles. His false nose looked like it had been broken at least a dozen times, and the bald cap wasn't fooling anyone. And where had he found that awful purple drape coat?

"Hello, Mr *Moriarty*? Would you care to take a seat?"

"Thank you. I don't mind if I do." His high-pitched voice was comical. "My knee has been giving me gyp all day."

"I'm so very sorry to hear that, Mr *Moriarty*."

"Are you alright, Mrs Maxwell?" He took a seat. "You seem rather — err — "

"I'm fine, thank you, Mr *Moriarty*. Now, tell me. What exactly is it that I can help you with?"

"I'm hoping that you'll be able to recover my stamp collection."

"*Stamp collection.*" I laughed. "Good one."

"Sorry?" He looked a little put out by my reaction. "Is there something funny about a stamp collection?"

"Not at all, Mr *Moriarty*, please do carry on. What exactly happened to your stamp collection?"

"I'm afraid it's been stolen."

"And I assume this stamp collection of yours is priceless?"

"No. In fact it has very little market value. It's priceless to me, though. I've spent over twenty-five years building it up."

"And you say it's been stolen." I laughed. "What self-respecting thief would waste their time with such a thing?"

"Really! I don't think you're taking—"

Just then my phone rang. "Excuse me, would you, Mr Moriarty?"

"Jill, it's me. Can you talk?"

"Martin?" I glanced back and forth between Mr Moriarty and my phone. "Where are you?"

"In Coffee Games."

"Are you sure? You're not sitting in my office?"

"Sorry?"

"Never mind. I'll have to call you back in a few minutes." I ended the call.

"Really, Mrs Maxwell." Mr Moriarty stood up. "I've never been treated so badly."

"Just a minute, please. I think there may have been a mistake."

"The only mistake was my coming here." He hobbled to the door. "I will make it my mission to warn everyone I know that you are not a person to do business with."

"But, Mr Moriarty—"

It was too late, he'd already left.

"Once again, your customer-facing skills come to the fore." Winky laughed.

"Shut it."

"Are you there, Moriarty?" He waved a rolled-up magazine around.

I threw the stapler at him, but he was too quick and dodged under the sofa.

Well, that was just great. I was desperate for new cases, so what do I do when a potential client walks through the door? I mock his name and insult him so badly that he storms back out. Truly brilliant.

"Martin, sorry about that. What did you want?"

"Something urgent has cropped up back in Candlefield. *My* Candlefield, that is. I'm probably going to be gone for a while, so I thought I should let you know."

"What's wrong?"

"Nothing I can't handle. I'll give you a bell when I get back."

"Okay. See you."

***

I'd just pulled onto my driveway and got out of the car when Norm Normal came rushing across the road towards me. He was waving his hands about, and he looked totally panic-stricken.

"Jill," he yelled. "Whatever you do, don't go inside your house."

"Why not? What's wrong, Norm?"

"There's something evil in there."

"I'm sorry. I have no idea what you're talking about."

"Naomi and I were walking down the street, and I just happened to glance over at your house. I wasn't being nosy, you understand, but I saw the most horrific creature standing by the window, staring out at me. I thought at first that I must be seeing things, but then Naomi saw it too. She was so shaken that she almost fainted."

Oh, bum!

"What kind of creature do you think you saw, Norm?"

"I realise this might sound crazy, but it looked like a zombie."

"*A zombie?*" I forced a laugh. "There's no such thing."

"I'm telling you, Jill, I saw it. I sent Naomi back to the house to call the police."

"What? No!" I rushed across the road to their house. Fortunately, Naomi had left the door open. When I got inside, she had the phone in her hand, so I hurried over, grabbed it, and killed the call.

"Jill, what are you doing?" She was clearly in a state of shock. "I was just about to call the police, to tell them about the zombie in your house."

"I'm sorry I was so rough, Naomi, but you don't know the full story."

"What *is* the full story, Jill?" Norm had joined us now, and he looked a little put out by what must have seemed like irrational behaviour on my part.

"What you saw just now isn't a zombie."

"But we both saw it, Jill."

"I'm sure you did. The thing is, I have a friend staying with me at the moment. He's an actor—only small parts up to now. Anyway, he's landed a walk-on part in a horror movie they're filming a few miles from here. What you saw was my friend in full costume and make-up. He probably nipped back from the set, to grab something to eat."

"What a relief." Naomi sighed. "I thought for a moment it was the end of the world, and we were about to be overrun by the undead. You must think we're such idiots."

"Not at all. Your reaction was perfectly understandable, but there really is nothing to worry about. Anyway, I must get back now because it's my turn to make dinner. I'll tell my friend to stay away from the window. We don't want him scaring the other neighbours, do we?"

I found Ike sitting at the kitchen table. For a zombie (lookalike), he looked very sheepish.

"I know what you're going to say, Jill, and I'm really sorry. I got so bored sitting in here that I thought I'd take a quick peep out of the window, but then your neighbours walked by and spotted me. What are they going to do? Have they called the authorities?"

"No. Luckily, I caught them before they could call the police, but it was a close thing."

"I really am sorry. Did you manage to update your spell book?"

"Not yet. I'll go and do it now. You stay here."

I went through to the lounge, grabbed the spell book, and sure enough, there on the back page, were the instructions on how to update it. It was a simple process that required me to cast a specific spell on the book. Unfortunately, when I did that, a message appeared informing me that my subscription had expired.

What subscription? No one ever mentioned a subscription to me.

The message went on to explain that the only way to renew it was by visiting the Spell Upgrades and Subscriptions Office in Candlefield, which was open between the hours of 9:30 and 15:30. It was already too late — they would be closed by now.

Great! Just great!

"I'm sorry, Ike, but I'm not going to be able to do anything today because the subscription on my spell book has run out."

"Can't you update it online?"

"I wish I could, but apparently I have to go to their

offices, which are closed until tomorrow morning. You're just going to have to stay here for another day, I'm afraid."

By the time Jack got home, I had dinner ready and waiting.

"Mmm." He gave me a peck on the cheek when I met him at the door. "Something smells good."

"It's your favourite: haddock, chips and mushy peas."

"Yummy. Can't wait." He followed me through to the kitchen, but then stopped dead in his tracks when he spotted Ike sitting at the table.

"Ike has to stay for another day," I said. "He's having dinner with us."

Jack still didn't move.

"Come on, your dinner will be cold." I tapped the chair next to me.

"Actually, I've lost my appetite."

Before I could respond, he'd backed out of the kitchen, and made for the stairs.

After I'd finished my dinner, I went in search of Jack who was in the bedroom.

"What's going on, Jack? I spent ages making that dinner."

"Sorry, but there's no way I could eat while sitting opposite a zombie. Just looking at that thing makes me want to throw up. I thought he would have gone by now."

"He should have, but I couldn't update the spell book because my subscription has run out. I have to get it renewed tomorrow."

"Fair enough. Are you sure you won't change your

mind about coming with us to TrainCon on Sunday?"

"Err, let me think about it. Spend all day with a bunch of people dressed as trains? It's tempting, but no."

"You might enjoy it."

"No, I wouldn't. You're already dragging me to one fancy dress party this weekend. Couldn't we cancel the community band thing now you're going to TrainCon?"

"No, we can't. We promised we'd be there. And besides, you're the star of the band. This weekend is going to be great. The fancy dress on Saturday night and TrainCon on Sunday. I can't wait."

"Me neither." Yawn.

Chapter 7

For some inexplicable reason, I woke up at a quarter to six the next morning. When I rolled over in bed, I realised that Jack had already got up. Why on earth would he be up so early? Was he ill?

I threw on my dressing gown and went to investigate. I found him at the kitchen table, halfway through a bowl of muesli.

"Do you have to go in early this morning, Jack? You didn't mention it last night."

"No, just the usual time."

"Then why are you up at stupid o'clock, eating muesli?"

"I was starving, and I wanted to get my breakfast before our friend upstairs woke up."

"I'm not surprised you're starving. You didn't eat any of the dinner I made for you last night."

"I couldn't. Not with you-know-who sitting opposite me. That's why I'm up so early this morning. I wanted to be able to enjoy my muesli without having to stare at the living dead. Speaking of whom, I haven't heard him moving around yet, have you?"

"Not yet. Maybe his legs fell off during the night."

"That's a horrible thing to say, Jill."

"It was only a joke. Sheesh."

"Would you like me to make you a fry up?" Jack offered.

"Err, no, thanks. To tell you the truth, I don't have much of an appetite. I'll just have a few corn flakes."

"You're not on a diet, are you? You certainly don't need to be."

"Of course I'm not."

"It's just that you don't seem to be eating very much recently."

"I'm not really hungry yet. I'll probably get something else later this morning."

After I'd poured myself some corn flakes, I joined him at the table.

"By the way, Jill, did you enquire about those ruby fairies?"

"Yes, I did. I meant to mention it last night."

"Before you fell asleep watching Netflix, you mean?"

"I wasn't sleeping. I was just resting my eyes."

"For two hours?"

"Do you want to know about the ruby fairies or not?"

"Sorry, go on. I'm all ears."

"It sounds quite promising. Apparently, you get paid so much per fairy per day. If we were to take one, we'd make about nine hundred pounds over the hibernation period."

"That's not bad." Jack nodded his approval.

"It gets even better. We're allowed to take a maximum of five of them. That means we'd make four and a half grand."

"Wow! And did they say we could do that?"

"Yes. The fairies should be here on Monday."

"It wasn't a problem that we live in the human world, then?"

"No, they didn't seem to care about that."

"What about the fact that I'm a human?"

"Err—no, that was okay too."

"Why do I get the impression there's something you're not telling me? You didn't lie and tell them I was a sup, did you?"

"Of course not. They just kind of assumed we were both

sups."

"And you didn't correct them?"

"I was going to, but I didn't get the chance. You'll just have to make sure that you aren't around when the fairies are delivered or collected. That way, they'll be none the wiser and everything will be sweet."

"And what exactly do we have to do while they're staying with us?"

"That's the best part. We don't have to do anything, other than provide them with a warm place to sleep. I thought we could clear a shelf in the airing cupboard and put them in there."

"What about food and drink?"

"They don't need either while they're hibernating. We just have to let them sleep here until the end of the hibernation period, when they'll be collected."

"That sounds almost too good to be true."

"It's right, though."

"And we'll get four and a half thousand pounds just for doing that?"

"Brilliant, isn't it? We'll be able to have a great holiday next year."

***

When I arrived at the office, the linen basket had been emptied and was lying on its side. Mrs V was just about to spray it with something.

"Morning, Jill. I've cleared out what was left of the yarn, and I'm going to spray the basket with this, which is guaranteed to get rid of all bugs. Hopefully, that will do the trick. I've also ordered some new yarn, which will be delivered later today. I hope you don't mind it being brought here."

"Of course not."

I was about to go through to my office when Mrs V called me back. "Jill, I had a phone call from a potential new client yesterday after you'd left."

"Did they say what it was about?"

"The lady's name is Mrs Harty. She wouldn't give me any details, other than to say it was related to the theft of something valuable. She's coming in later this morning."

"That's great, thanks."

In my office, Winky was running around like a crazy cat. I was just about to ask him what he was doing when I realised that he was chasing something. That *something* was a huge, ugly creepy-crawly with lots of legs. Winky pounced, caught it in his paws, and dropped it into a jam jar, before screwing on the lid.

"What's that, Winky?"

"What's *what*?" He shrugged.

"That thing in the jam jar."

"Oh, that thing. That's Ivan."

"And what exactly is *Ivan*?"

"A bug. Well, a superbug, to be precise."

"And how long have you had Ivan?"

"Just a few days."

"Out of curiosity, what does Ivan like to eat?"

"Oh, you know. This and that."

"Is it possible that *this and that* could include yarn?"

"I believe he's quite partial to yarn, yes."

"I thought as much. He's the one that's been eating Mrs V's yarn, isn't he?"

"I suppose it's possible." Winky shrugged. "I had to let him out during the night for some exercise, and I can't be sure what he was doing while I was asleep."

"You did this deliberately. You knew that he'd eat Mrs V's yarn."

"Of course I didn't. I had no idea that would happen."

"Where does Ivan come from, anyway?"

"I'm looking after him for a friend, Billy the Bugs. He had to go and see his poor old mum in hospital. He'll be away for a few days, so he asked some of his friends to look after his collection of bugs. I volunteered to look after Ivan."

"That thing has destroyed all of Mrs V's yarn, and it's going to cost her a small fortune to replace it. If anything happens to the new batch, which is being delivered later today, I'll stomp on Ivan, and then I'll stomp on you."

***

Although the ruby fairy foster scheme would help with our finances, what I really needed was an influx of new clients and cases. That's why I was determined to impress Mrs Harty.

"Good morning, Mrs Harty," I said, in my best customer-facing voice. "Do have a seat."

"Thank you, and please call me Lori."

Lori? That would make her Lori Harty, which rhymed with Moriarty.

Was someone trying to wind me up again?

Hang on. I reminded myself what had happened with Mr Moriarty when I'd thought he was Martin, trying to prank me. My rude manner had caused Moriarty to walk out in disgust. I couldn't afford a repetition of that.

"Mrs Maxwell?" Lori had obviously realised that I'd zoned out. "Are you okay?"

"Sorry, Lori. Please call me Jill. Can I get you a drink?"

"Not for me, thanks. I'd prefer to get straight down to business if it's all the same to you."

"Absolutely. How exactly can I help you today?"

"Something rather valuable has been stolen from me."

"Was it a stamp collection, by any chance?"

"*Stamp collection*?" She gave me a puzzled look. "No, I have no interest in stamps. It's a painting."

"I see. And it's valuable, you say?"

"Yes. Not Picasso/van Gogh type valuable, but it did cost me over twenty thousand. I've only had it for a few days."

"Where was it stolen from?"

"My apartment. I'm actually a bit of a collector. I have over twenty paintings in total. This one was my favourite, though."

"And the most valuable?"

"By some considerable margin, yes."

"Do you keep them all in your apartment?"

"Yes, they're all on display. I'm not one of those people who believe in storing art away from view. I like to be able to appreciate them every day."

"How was the painting stolen? Was there a burglary?"

"That's the weird thing. I don't know how it happened."

"Can you talk me through what you do know?"

"Of course. I'm a member of the Washbridge Fine Art Appreciation Society, or WFAAS for short. It's a very small society; there are only five of us altogether. We meet once a month at each other's homes. On this particular day, it was my turn to host the get-together. I'd gone into the kitchen to make drinks when I heard a strange buzzing noise coming from the next room. I didn't think much of it at the time, but when I took the drinks through, everyone was in a state of panic because the room was full of bees."

"Bumblebees?"

"That's right. We had no choice but to abandon the meeting. We left the apartment, went downstairs, and I called the pest control man. The others went home while I waited in the garden for him to arrive. I'd assumed there must be a bees' nest somewhere, but after the pest control man had cleared the bees out of the apartment, he conducted a thorough search, but found no trace of one. When I went back up to my apartment, the painting had gone."

"Is it possible that the pest control man took it?"

"No. I watched him leave. The only thing he was carrying was a small tool kit, much too small to accommodate the painting."

"What about the other members of your group? Could any of those have taken it?"

"No, because I walked out of the apartment with them, and I'd have seen it. The three ladies only had handbags with them, and they certainly weren't large enough to conceal the painting. And Finley didn't have a bag with him at all."

"Finley?"

"Yes. He's the only man in our little group."

"Was the painting definitely there when you began the meeting?"

"Yes, when I sat at the head of the table, it was on the wall directly in front of me."

"But it had gone by the time you returned to the apartment after the pest control man had got rid of the bees?"

"That's correct."

"Are you sure it was there before you went to make the drinks?"

"Absolutely."

"What about when you returned with the drinks? Can you be sure if it was still there then?"

"No, as I mentioned before, everyone was freaking out because of the bees. People were running around, trying to swat them away, and then we all left the building."

"Have you reported the theft to the police?"

"Yes, that was the first thing I did. They sent a young constable over to see me. He took a few notes, but to be honest, I got the impression that they were unlikely to put much by way of resources into it. He did say they'd keep me posted, and that there had been lots of other burglaries in the area. I'm not very hopeful, which is why I'm here today."

"I'd like to start by paying a visit to your apartment if that's possible, so I can see the room where the painting was being kept."

"That's fine. Come around any time. Oh, and one other thing I forgot to mention: the apartment block has CCTV throughout the building, and on both the front and rear entrances. I told security that I intended to hire a private investigator, and they said that you'd be welcome to look at the footage if you think it would be helpful."

"That's great. There's just one more thing I need from

you, Lori. Can you let me have a list of the other members of your art appreciation group?"

"Certainly. I'll do that before I leave, but as I said, I'm absolutely sure they aren't responsible for the theft. If any of them had been carrying the painting, I'd have seen it."

A few minutes after Lori had left, the door to my office flew open and in walked someone wearing what appeared to be a beekeeper's hat. I had no idea who it was because they had the mesh pulled down in front of their face.

"Can I help you?" I said.

"You most certainly can."

"Grandma? Why are you wearing a beekeeper's hat?"

"I'll show you why." She lifted up the mesh.

"Oh no! What happened to your wart? It's huge."

"Is it really? Thanks for pointing that out because I hadn't noticed." She rolled her eyes. "Why else do you think I'm wearing this stupid hat?"

"Didn't the potion that Rhonda Rules recommended work?"

"The wart is no longer flashing red, yellow and green, so I suppose it worked in that respect, but this is hardly an improvement, is it? I can barely see over the top of this thing."

Before I could stop myself, I laughed.

"This is not funny!"

"Sorry, I know it isn't." I somehow managed to compose myself. "Perhaps it's just a side effect."

"Of course it's a side effect. That doesn't make it any better."

"You're right, but I'm not sure what you want me to do

about it."

"I'd have thought that was quite obvious. I want you to find Rhonda, tell her what's happened, and tell her that if she doesn't sort this out, I will personally go over there and kick her backside."

"Wouldn't it be better if you went to see her yourself?"

"No, it would not. I don't want anyone to see me looking like this. It's bad enough that I had to come up here to see you. I tried calling you, but I got no response."

"Sorry. I had the sound turned down on my phone because I had a client with me."

"Well, what are you waiting for?"

"You want me to go over there right now?"

"Of course I do. And you'd better look sharp, girl." With that, she stormed out of the office.

Poor old Grandma. She drove me crazy, but I wouldn't have wished that wart on anyone.

Chapter 8

I was just about to magic myself over to Candlefield in search of Rhonda Rules when I received a phone call.

"Is that Jill Maxwell?"

"Jill Maxwell speaking."

"It's Harvey Baskerville from Harvey's Booksheller."

"Hi there. Do you have news for me?"

"Yes, I do. I've actually found two copies."

"That's great. When can I call in to collect one?"

"Anytime, but I wanted to let you know that one of the copies has been signed by the author himself. Obviously, the price I quoted you of twenty-five pounds still stands for the unsigned edition, but I thought I'd better check in case your friend, Mr Rhymes, would prefer to pay extra to have the signed edition. I don't mind either way."

"I'll need to check with Rhymes. How much would the signed edition be?"

"I'd want sixty pounds for that one."

"Okay. I'll call on Rhymes later today, and then pop into the shop. What time do you close today?"

"Not until five o'clock."

"I'll see you later, then."

Before I could go and see Rhymes, I needed to find Rhonda Rules, to try and sort out Grandma's wart problem.

The Three Merry Turkeys was one establishment that I'd hoped never to return to.

"Hello again, Missy." The man behind the counter still hadn't had a shave. "You're becoming a regular in here."

Not by choice, that was for sure.

"I need to see Rhonda again. Is she upstairs?"

"Not today. She's in the kitchen, making herself a snack."

"Right. Is it okay to go through and have a quick word with her?"

"Feel free. It's the first door on the right."

It was with some trepidation that I made my way through to the kitchen. I found it hard to believe that this dump actually offered food.

Even though the kitchen wasn't as bad as I'd expected, I wouldn't be ordering any food from there any time soon. Standing by the microwave, Rhonda hadn't noticed me come in.

"Hello again, Rhonda."

She looked at me but showed no sign of recognition. "Do I know you?"

"I'm Jill Maxwell. I came to see you yesterday."

The microwave pinged, and she took out what looked like a bowl of macaroni cheese. Normally, I love mac and cheese, but for some reason, the smell turned my stomach.

"Sorry, I don't remember that," she said.

"You were upstairs. I had to wake you up, to ask you for help with my grandmother, Mirabel Millbright."

"That does ring a bell, but I thought it was a dream. Was it something to do with her nose?"

"That's right. It was turning from red, to yellow, to green."

"That sounds like traffic light nose syndrome."

"That's what you said yesterday."

"I did? Thank goodness. For a moment there, I was worried I might've given you the wrong advice."

"You suggested a potion for her to use."

"Did it stop the TLN syndrome?"

"Yes, it did."

"Excellent."

"Not really. It seems to have caused another problem. The wart has grown much larger; it's now almost as big as her head."

"Oh, no." Rhonda looked horrified. "I don't imagine Mirabel is best pleased about that."

"You're right. She isn't."

"What potion did I suggest that she use?"

"Rat hair and thistle."

"Are you sure that's what I said?"

"Positive. Why?"

"It's not *rat* hair and thistle that she needs. It's *bat* hair and thistle. Is it possible you misheard me?"

"I don't think so. What can we do about it?"

"You need to go back to the apothecary, purchase some bat hair and thistle, and have your grandmother apply it three times a day, but tell her to use twice the normal recommended dose. That should sort out the problem within a matter of three to four days."

"That long? She's not going to be very happy about that."

"I'm sure she won't, but I'm afraid it's the best I can do. Nothing else is going to sort it out any quicker."

"Okay. Thanks, Rhonda. I'd better get over there now."

In the apothecary, Patricia was on duty again.

"Hi, did the potion you bought yesterday do the trick?"

"Not exactly. There's seems to have been some kind of mix up. Apparently, what I needed wasn't *rat* hair and thistle, it was *bat* hair and thistle."

"I must admit that when you asked for rat hair, I did think it was rather unusual, but I didn't like to argue with Rhonda. She is the expert on these matters, after all."

"Do you have any bat hair and thistle potion?"

"Let me go and check for you."

She slid the ladder across the room, then climbed the steps.

"Oh, dear. I think we may be all out of it."

My heart sank.

"Wait a minute. There's one right at the back. Let me see if I can reach it. Got it! I'm afraid it's a little dusty. I'd better check the best before date. You're okay; it's got another year to run." She climbed down the ladder, handed me the potion, and I gave her another fifteen pounds.

Potion in hand, I magicked myself back to Washbridge.

Julie was on duty in Ever, and she looked even more cheesed off than usual.

"Hi, Julie. Not having a good day, I take it?"

"Terrible. It's your grandmother. I don't know what's wrong with her, but she's even worse than usual. She's been walking around all day, wearing a beekeeper's hat, and she's been in a foul mood. Every time I've spoken to her, she's nearly bitten my head off."

"You shouldn't have to put up with that. Not for the money she pays you."

"Between you and me, Jill," she said in a whisper, "and please don't tell your grandmother, but I'm looking for another job. I can't stand this place any longer."

"Don't worry. I won't say anything. And to be honest, I don't blame you. Anyway, I'd better go and see her."

Grandma was seated at her desk, still wearing the beekeeper's hat.

"What did Rhonda have to say for herself?" she snapped. "What excuse did she come up with for doing this to me?"

"Actually, Grandma, I'm not sure that it was entirely Rhonda's fault."

"What do you mean? She was the one who told you to buy this potion, wasn't she?"

"It's possible I may have misheard what she said."

"*Misheard*?" she exploded. "Are you telling me that I have to put up with this thing because you *misheard* her?" She lifted the flap to reveal the wart, which was now even larger.

"I'm really sorry. Apparently, what you need is bat hair and thistle, but what I bought was rat hair and thistle."

"Well, that's just dandy, and how does Rhonda propose to sort this out?"

"I've got the bat hair and thistle potion." I held up the jar. "Rhonda says if you apply this three times a day, using twice the recommended dose, that will resolve the problem."

"It better had."

"There's just one more thing, Grandma."

"What?"

"Rhonda said it would take three to four days."

"I can't walk around looking like this for another three to four days."

"I'm really sorry, but according to Rhonda, there's nothing that will sort it out any quicker."

"What are you waiting for, then?"

"Sorry, I don't know what you mean."

"I need you to put the potion on the wart for me."

"Me?"

"I don't see anyone else in here, and I can't reach around the front of it myself. Come on, girl, hurry up."

"Okay." When I unscrewed the jar, the smell was truly awful, and I thought for a moment that I was going to be sick, but I somehow managed to keep it down.

After dipping my fingers into the horrible green-brown mush, I began to apply it to her wart.

When I'd finished, I said goodbye to Grandma and rushed to the staffroom, to wash my hands.

"Are you okay, Jill?" Julie had followed me inside.

"Not really."

"What's that awful smell?"

"It's—err—some lotion that Grandma asked me to get for her. Whatever you do, Julie, don't go into her office today. If you do, you'll regret it."

I spent over fifteen minutes washing and re-washing my hands until I was sure they no longer smelled of that awful potion. Only then, did I magic myself over to Candlefield.

I wanted to renew my subscription so that I'd be able to update my spell book. It turned out that the office I needed was inside the town hall. The place was like a labyrinth, but I eventually found the office in question. Behind the counter stood a tall, slim wizard with an unusual quiff.

"Good day, madam, how can I be of assistance?"

"I'd like to renew the subscription for my spell book, so that I can update it. Am I in the right place?"

"You are, indeed, madam."

"Apparently, my subscription lapsed some time ago. I hadn't even realised I needed one."

"The information is all there on the back page, madam. It's very clear."

"Yes, I realise it's my fault. Anyway, could I renew the subscription?"

"You understand that you'll have to pay for the period during which it had lapsed, as well as for the new period, don't you?"

"I didn't, but fair enough."

"We just need to fill out the paperwork." He reached under the counter and produced a form. "First, if I could have your name, please?"

"Jill Maxwell."

"And the registration number of your book?"

"Registration number?"

"I need that in order to renew your subscription."

"I don't know what it is."

"I'm afraid without that it's impossible for me to process your request because the subscription is tied to the registration number."

"I see, and where would I find the registration number?"

"That too is on the back page of the book, madam. It's in the bottom left corner, in small print. You'll know it because it says, registration number, and then there's a number."

I really didn't appreciate his sarcasm, but I didn't want to get in his bad books, so I let it slide on this occasion.

"In that case, I'd better go and find out what it is. What time do you close today?"

He glanced up at the clock on the wall. "In about two

minutes' time."

"I thought you were open until five."

"No, madam. We close at three-thirty."

"Three-thirty? That's the middle of the afternoon. I wish I could get a job like yours."

"Was there something else, madam?"

"No. I guess I'll just have to come back tomorrow."

Great! That meant Ike was going to have to stay with us for another night. He wouldn't be very pleased, and Jack certainly wouldn't. He'd no doubt decide to give dinner a miss again. At this rate, Jack would have lost half a stone by the time Ike finally left.

***

I needed to find out from Rhymes whether or not he wanted the signed copy of the book. When I arrived outside at Aunt Lucy's house, I could hear a wailing sound coming from inside. I let myself in and found Aunt Lucy in the lounge with her new neighbours, the two werewolves. The young woman was holding a baby in her arms.

"Hi there, Jill," Aunt Lucy had to shout over the screaming baby.

"Hi."

"Bea and Ben came over to show me their new baby, Lee. Isn't he gorgeous?"

The baby looked like every other baby I'd ever seen, apart from the fact that he was huge.

"Yes, he's gorgeous," I said. "He certainly has some lungs on him, doesn't he?"

"That's for sure," said his proud mother. "Would you like to hold him?"

Before I could decline, she'd already passed him to me.

"Hello, there," I said. "Goo, goo, goo."

The baby stopped crying, looked up at me, and cracked a smile.

"You certainly have a way with babies," Ben said. "We should get you to come around in the evenings, to put him to bed for us."

"I always said you'd make a great mum." Aunt Lucy grinned.

I held the baby just long enough to be polite, then handed him back. Curiously, as soon as he was back in his mother's arms, he began to wail again.

"I only popped over to see Rhymes," I shouted to Aunt Lucy. "I'll just nip upstairs and have a quick word with him."

As soon as I walked into the back bedroom, Barry came bounding over to me.

"Do you need any jobs doing, Jill?"

"Not really, Barry. I don't live here, remember."

"I could come over to your house and clean that."

"I don't think that's a good idea. You didn't like it the last time you were there, remember?"

"Look what I've got, though." He used his paw to nudge the medal that was hanging around his neck.

"Where's that from, boy?"

"I got it from the Dog Scouts for doing a good deed every day for the last week. Do you like it, Jill?"

"It's very nice. You should be proud of yourself."

"I am, but I want to get another one, so I need to find a job to do every day."

"I'm sure Aunt Lucy will come up with something. Is Rhymes here?"

"He's under the bed."

I got down on all fours and found the little tortoise, still looking rather sorry for himself.

"Hi, Rhymes," I shouted.

"Hi, Jill. I didn't see you there."

"I came about that book you wanted me to find."

"It's okay. I didn't really expect you to find it."

"Actually, I have."

"Really?" His little face lit up.

"Yes. In fact, the shop has two copies. One of them is unsigned and costs twenty-five pounds, but they also have a signed copy, which is sixty pounds. I wanted to check which one you'd rather have."

He thought about it for a moment. "Sixty pounds is a lot of money, isn't it?"

"That's what I thought. Shall I get the unsigned one?"

"No. I have some savings put by, and now that I'm not seeing Poesy anymore, I won't be spending much money on anything else, so, I might as well have the signed copy, please."

"Are you sure about that?"

"Yes, please." He reached inside his shell and brought out a wad of notes. "Twenty, forty, sixty pounds. There you are, Jill."

"Okay. I'll go get it and drop it off later. Oh, and the man in the shop said if you let him have some copies of your book, he'll try to sell them for you."

"Did he, really?" Rhymes' little face lit up. "That's fantastic. I'll sign a few for you to give to him."

Chapter 9

There was little wonder that my business wasn't doing very well. I seemed to spend half of my time running around after other people. Take today, for example: I'd been back and forth to Candlefield, trying to sort out Grandma's wart, and then I'd had to search for a rare book for my tortoise. Granted, a lot of that time had been spent in Candlefield, so time had stood still in the human world, but it was still exhausting. I wasn't just running a private investigation business; I was also providing a concierge service.

Not that I was complaining, obviously.

Meanwhile, back on the Kramer case, I figured I ought to find out a little more about Alison Reed—the young woman who had been poisoned and for whose murder Arnold Kramer had been convicted.

I'd managed to track down Alison Reed's flatmate, a woman who, at the time of the poisoning, had been called Paula Frice. Having subsequently married, her name was now Paula Conway. She and her new husband, Richard, were living at her parents' house while they saved enough money to put down a deposit on a place of their own.

How did I know all of this? Because she'd spent the last fifteen minutes telling me her life story. We were in her bedroom; the one she now shared with her husband, at her parents' house.

"Richard says that if we carry on saving like this, we'll have enough for a deposit in about a year," Paula said.

"That's great." I did my best to sound as though I cared. "It'll be nice for you to have your own place."

"Tell me about it. I know it's good of Mum and Dad to let us stay here, but Mum is seriously doing my head in. She still thinks I'm fourteen, but I'm twenty-seven now. And Dad doesn't get along with Richard at all; they're always arguing."

"It must be very difficult. Anyway, you were going to tell me about Alison."

"Oh yes. Poor Ali. That upset me for months, you know. I still think about her every day."

"How long were you and she flatmates?"

"Not long. Just under two years."

"Had you known each other before that?"

"Yes. She used to live a couple of streets from here, and we were at school together. When we both got jobs, we decided we'd share a flat. It wasn't up to much; a glorified bedsit, if I'm honest, but it was better than having to live with our parents."

"What kind of person was Alison?"

"She — err — " Paula hesitated.

"Go on, please. Just be honest."

"I don't want to speak ill of the dead."

"I understand that, but it's important that I find out exactly what happened."

"She and I got along okay, but the truth is, she used people. Men, in particular."

"Used them how?"

"Have you seen photos of Alison?"

I nodded.

"Then you'll know she was beautiful. She could pick up guys without even trying; all she had to do was flash that smile of hers. She'd go out with them for a few weeks, get them to pay for her on nights out, buy her presents, that kind of thing. Then she'd dump them."

"Is that what happened with Arnold?"

"Yes. From what I can remember, he didn't last very long at all. Probably not much more than a couple of weeks. She told me that he was super boring, and that he didn't have any money. I felt really sorry for the guy. He wasn't like the men that Alison usually went out with. Most of them were players themselves, so when she dumped them, they didn't much care. They just moved on to the next girl. Arnold was smitten. I wouldn't have been surprised if Alison was his first girlfriend."

"Did you see Arnold again after he and Alison split up?"

"Yes, just the once. He came over to the flat to see her, but she wasn't in. He said he wanted to try and patch things up. I told him he was wasting his time and that Alison had already found someone else."

"How did he take that? Was he angry?"

"No, he just looked upset; I thought he was going to cry. It was a bit embarrassing, to be honest."

"What did you think when you heard that Arnold had been charged with Alison's murder?"

"I was gobsmacked. He didn't strike me as the type to be capable of something like that, but then you never know with people, do you? They always say the quiet ones are the worst, don't they?"

"Is there anyone else you can think of who might have wanted to hurt Alison?"

"She definitely upset a lot of people. She was always very outspoken, not the kind to turn the other cheek. If someone said something she didn't like, she'd let them have both barrels. Having said that, I can't think of anyone who'd want to physically hurt her."

***

After I'd left Paula Conway's house, I decided to call it a day and head home. As soon as I walked through the door, Ike came rushing out of the kitchen to greet me. Although I knew he wasn't really a zombie, it was still unnerving to have the undead rushing towards you.

"Did you manage to get your subscription updated, Jill?"

"I'm afraid not. Apparently, they need the registration number of my spell book, and I didn't have it with me."

"Couldn't you just go back there again now?"

"It wouldn't do any good. They were closing just as I left. I'll have to try again tomorrow."

"Oh, no!" He sighed. "I don't know if I can bear another day here."

"Charming."

"Sorry, Jill. I don't mean to sound ungrateful. I really do appreciate everything you've done for me, but my wife has probably started to worry now."

"I didn't realise you were married. Wouldn't she have been worried long before now?"

"Not necessarily. Because of the nature of the work I do, I'm often away for one or two nights at a stretch, but if I'm not back tonight, she'll hit the panic button."

"Couldn't you give her a call?"

"I don't have my phone with me. I was in such a panic when this happened that I rushed out without it. I don't suppose I could borrow yours, could I?"

I looked at his bony, flaky hands, and hesitated. "Err—

yeah, I guess so."

"Thanks, Jill. I'll go and give her a call. I'm sorry if I was short with you just now. It's just that this is all very frustrating."

"Don't give it another thought."

I was worried about how Jack would react when he discovered that Ike was going to be with us for another night. He'd probably go crazy.

I'd just got changed when I heard him come through the door. I wanted to catch him before he saw Ike, so I hurried down the stairs.

"Jack, could I have a quiet word with you in the lounge?"

"Err, okay." He looked a little puzzled. "What's wrong?"

"I'm afraid Ike's going to be staying with us for another night."

"Oh? How come?"

"I wasn't able to renew my subscription, so I couldn't update the spell book. I'm going to have to try again tomorrow."

"Don't worry about it. It's not a problem."

That wasn't the reaction I'd expected.

"I thought having Ike here might put you off your dinner."

"It definitely would, so why don't you and I go out for dinner somewhere?"

"Can we afford it?"

"We can now that we're going to foster the ruby fairies. What do you say?"

"Sure. I'd be up for that, but I don't want to go to that

stupid train restaurant again."

"Of course not." He laughed. "You can pick where we go. It'll be my treat."

"Okay, I'll give it some thought while I get changed."

Upstairs, while I was trying to decide where we should eat, I couldn't help but wonder what had got into Jack. I'd expected him to be furious when I told him that Ike would be staying for another night, but he'd taken it all in his stride, and he'd even offered to take me out for dinner.

Did he have an ulterior motive?

Of course he didn't. Why did I always have to be so suspicious of everyone? He was doing it because he loved me.

I eventually decided on a little restaurant, which we'd been to once before, called Washbridge Kitchen. Jack had insisted on ordering a taxi, so that we could both have a drink if we wanted one. We hadn't bothered to book because restaurants around there were rarely busy midweek.

"What's going on?" Jack said when we walked into the restaurant.

The place was deserted. I'd expected it to be quiet, but not *this* quiet.

A waiter spotted us and came over.

"It looks like you have plenty of free tables," I said.

"I'm very sorry, madam, but we won't be serving food tonight."

"Why not?"

"The cold-room broke down a couple of hours ago. We've called the repair man, but he can't get here until the morning. You're welcome to have a drink at the bar, and I can book you a table for tomorrow if you like."

"Err, no thanks. We'll give it a miss."

A little disappointed, we went instead to a small pizza restaurant in the next street. As it turned out, we struck lucky because the pizza was delicious, and we both made short work of it.

"Do you want a pudding?" Jack asked.

"Just a couple of scoops of ice cream, I think."

"Are you sure that's all you want? They have some fantastic desserts."

"Ice cream will be fine."

After we'd finished dessert, Jack said, "I really enjoyed this evening. We should do it more often."

"Actually, we're dining out two days next week. We're going out with Luther and Rebecca on Monday, and then on Thursday, we're seeing Swotty Dotty and her partner."

"I hope you're not going to call her that on the day." He grinned.

"Of course I won't. It's just force of habit."

"Oh yes, there's something I wanted to mention to you, Jill. Peter rang earlier today. He and Mikey are going go-karting on Saturday, and he asked if I'd like to go with them."

"Ah, now it all becomes clear."

"Sorry?"

"That explains everything. Why you weren't upset when I told you that Ike would be staying for another day. And why you suggested we go out for a meal. You were trying to butter me up, so you can go go-karting."

"That's not true," he protested. "The thought never entered my head."

"You're such a bad liar, Jack. Look, I don't mind if you want to go. Just don't crash and put yourself in hospital."

"Thanks, Jill." He gave me a kiss. "You're the best."

"You're right. I am."

"You could go shopping with Kathy."

"I doubt it. She'll more than likely be working in the shop. Don't worry, I'll find something to pass the time."

"By the way, how's your grandmother's nose?"

"Not very good, I'm afraid. The potion sorted out the colour changing problem, but it's caused the wart to expand. It's twice as big as it was before."

He laughed. "I don't imagine she's very pleased about that."

"She was fuming. When she came to see me, she was wearing a beekeeper's hat to hide it."

"What can you do about it?"

"I had to get her another potion."

"Poor you."

"You haven't heard the worst part. She made me apply the potion to the wart."

"Thank goodness you didn't tell me that before we started to eat." He shuddered. "Do you think it'll cure it?"

"I certainly hope so. Otherwise I'm never going to hear the end of it."

Chapter 10

Jack and I had both skipped breakfast.

I didn't feel like eating anything, and Jack said he didn't want to risk his muesli being interrupted by the living dead. Before I went to work, I needed to pick up a few things from The Corner Shop.

The pile of baskets wasn't in its usual place, next to the door, so I walked over to the counter where Little Jack seemed to be having some difficulty. He was holding onto the wall for dear life, and his hair was blowing all over the place.

"Are you all right back there, Jack?"

"I think I may have the fan on the wrong setting," he shouted.

It was only then that I realised what the problem was. He'd installed a giant industrial fan behind the counter, and it was blowing a gale.

"What's with the fan, Jack?" I said.

"It gets so hot back here behind the glass screen that I had to do something. I had hoped the fan might cool it down, but I don't think I've got the settings quite right yet. Hold on there for a minute, Jill. I'll try and adjust it."

He released his grip on the counter and then started to walk, on his stilts, towards the fan. It was clearly hard going, and he looked like he was battling through a wind tunnel. Eventually, though, he reached the fan, turned the knob and adjusted the speed.

"That's better. Was there something you needed, Jill?"

"I can't find the baskets; they're not in the usual place."

"Unfortunately, I've had to introduce some security

measures because when I did an inventory last week, I discovered that ten percent of the baskets had gone missing. That's why I've installed that." He pointed to a strange looking machine just the other side of the door.

"How does it work?"

"You put a pound coin in the slot on the side. A basket will then come out of the large drawer at the bottom. When you've finished your shopping, simply put the basket back into the drawer, and the pound coin will be refunded."

"Okay, I'll give it a shot." I took a pound coin from my purse, dropped it in the slot, and sure enough, a basket appeared.

It only took me a few minutes to get everything I needed.

"No custard creams today, Jill?" Jack said, as he took my money.

"No, I still have plenty left, thanks."

"Are you cutting down on them? You're not on a diet, are you?"

"No, of course not."

"Okay, if you pop your basket back in the drawer, your pound coin will be refunded."

I went over to the machine and did as he said. My pound coin dropped into the tray. Then another one dropped into it. And another. They kept on coming until the tray was full of them, and then they started spilling out onto the floor.

"Jack! I think you may have a problem with this machine."

***

I'd dropped my shopping back at the house, and was just about to leave when Ike called to me from upstairs.

"Have you got the registration number of your spell book, Jill?"

Oh bum! I'd forgotten all about that.

"Yes, I've got it. Don't worry." I hurried into the lounge, jotted down the number, and then set off for work.

As I approached the office building, I stopped dead in my tracks because I'd seen something that I never thought I'd ever see. There, on the wall, was a sign. And not just any old sign. My sign! It had the correct wording; it looked to be the correct size, and it *wasn't* upside down. Result!

I skipped all the way to the office and up the stairs.

"Jill, you're looking very pleased with life." It was Jimmy who was standing with Kimmy.

"Hello, you two. I most certainly am. Did you see they've put up my sign at long last? I can't believe it. I've been waiting weeks for that."

"We noticed it on our way in. It looks really good."

"Thanks."

"We were going to come and see you later today."

"Oh?"

"Our first intake of clowns has just finished their course, and they'll be graduating next week."

"Do clown's graduate?"

"Of course they do. Just like any other students."

"O—kay."

"Anyway, we wanted to warn you that the graduation ceremony is next Tuesday, here at our offices, and there'll probably be a lot more clowns around on that day. I hope that'll be okay?"

"Of course it will. I don't have any problem with that kind of thing. It was just the permanent sign at the top of the stairs that I objected to. I hope the day goes well for you."

"Thanks, Jill."

Jimmy and Kimmy went on their way, and I headed into the office.

"Have you seen it, Mrs V? The sign?"

"Yes, Jill." She beamed. "I most certainly have."

"Doesn't it look great? When did they put it up?"

"They'd almost finished by the time I arrived. They must have started at the crack of dawn."

"I can't believe it's finally up. Maybe business will start to pick up now that people actually know we're here."

"Let's hope so, dear."

***

I'd telephoned the four other members of WFAAS, and they'd all agreed to talk to me.

First up, was a lady by the name of Hannah Westbrook, who lived in an apartment in the city centre.

"Thank you for seeing me, Mrs Westbrook."

"My pleasure. Do come in. I was just about to make a pot of green tea. Would you care for some?"

"Would it be possible to have a glass of water instead?"

"I don't have any in, I'm afraid."

"I meant from the tap."

"I suppose so. Are you sure?"

"Yes, please."

Moments later, she returned from the kitchen. She was holding my glass of water at arm's length, as though it was some kind of toxic substance.

"As I mentioned on the phone, Mrs Westbrook, I've been hired by Lori Harty to investigate the theft of her painting. Are you familiar with the item in question?"

"I am indeed. It's a nice enough piece of work, but not worth the amount of money she paid for it."

"Do you remember seeing it during the last meeting of WFAAS?"

"I'm not sure. Lori does have an awful lot of art on her walls. Too much, in fact. For me, less is more. As you can see, I have just the three paintings in this room, and I think that works rather nicely. Lori must have at least ten in her dining room, which I find a little overwhelming."

"Perhaps you could talk me through the events of that day?"

"There's not much to tell. We all arrived at the usual time, talked about this and that for a few minutes, then Lori went through to the kitchen to make drinks. That's when the bees appeared."

"Do you know where they came from?"

"Through the patio door, I assume. By the time Lori returned with the drinks, one of the horrible creatures had stung me." She pointed to her arm. "Then, we all hurried out of the apartment and down the stairs."

"What happened next?"

"Not much. There was no point in hanging around, so the four of us left. I believe Lori was going to wait in the garden for the pest control man to arrive."

"Do you have any idea who might have taken the

painting, Mrs Westbrook?"

"None at all. Although, I did hear that there had been a number of burglaries in that area recently."

* * *

Myrtle Turtle had been in touch to say that Walter Staniforth, the detective who'd been in charge of the Kramer case, had agreed to talk to me.

I'd arranged to meet Myrtle at her house, the old watermill. Middle Tweaking was a sleepy little village, and every time I paid it a visit, I pondered the possibility of Jack and me living there. Jack would love it, but I wasn't sure if I was cut out for village life; I might end up climbing the walls after a few months.

It was Hodd who answered the door.

"Well, well, well. If it isn't the private investigator. How are you, Jill?"

"Very well, thanks. Is Myrtle in?"

"Yes, come in. She's upstairs doing something with her drawers, I believe."

"She is expecting me."

"Yeah, she said you'd be popping over. I'll nip upstairs and tell her you're here."

No sooner had Hodd disappeared than Jobbs came out of the kitchen. "Hi, Jill. I was just about to make a drink. Would you like one?"

"That would be lovely, thanks."

"We have coffee, Earl Grey, and a selection of those poncy fruit teas, which Myrtle insists on buying."

"Earl Grey would be lovely, thanks."

Moments later, Hodd came back downstairs, followed

closely by Myrtle.

"I'm sorry to keep you waiting, Jill," Myrtle said. "I've been sorting out the cupboards in the bedroom. I don't know how I managed to accumulate so much rubbish. Would you like a drink?"

"Jobbs is making one for me, thanks."

"In that case, let's take the weight off our feet, and you can tell me all about the cases you've been working on recently. We'll go and talk to Walter after we've had our drinks."

Over tea, I talked the three of them through some of my recent cases.

"You certainly land your fair share of *interesting* cases," Hodd said.

"What about you three? Have you been up to anything interesting recently? Any part-time sleuthing?"

"I'm afraid not." Myrtle sighed. "Things have been even quieter than usual here in Middle Tweaking. It's a pity because I do like to keep my hand in with a little detective work on the side, but there's precious little opportunity here."

After we'd finished our drinks, Myrtle sent Hodd and Jobbs on their way, and she accompanied me to Walter Staniforth's. He lived in a small cottage on the northern edge of the village.

"I should warn you, Jill, even though Walter has agreed to talk to you, I got the impression that he wasn't a big fan of private investigators."

"That's okay. I'm used to policemen not having much time for me. My husband, Jack, felt exactly the same when we first met."

"You clearly managed to win him over." She laughed. "I get the feeling that Walter is finding retirement a little boring. That's probably why he agreed to talk to you."

Myrtle hammered on the door with the brass knocker. Moments later, a tall well-built man with a thick grey moustache, answered the door.

"Hello, Myrtle. And you must be Jill. Myrtle's told me a lot about you."

"Not all bad, I hope."

"No. In fact, she was singing your praises, and she doesn't do that about many people. Why don't you both come in?"

"I won't if you don't mind, Walter," Myrtle said. "I'm in the middle of tidying the bedroom, and besides, it'll be better if you and Jill discuss the case alone. If I'm there, I'll only go sticking my oar in."

"As you wish," Walter said.

"Thanks again, Myrtle." I gave her a little wave as she started back down the road.

There was something about the sitting room that made me suspect he lived alone. The top of the sideboard was covered in framed photographs: no partner or children in sight. Most of them were of Walter, taken while he was in the force.

"How long were you with the police, Walter?"

"All of my working life. I joined straight from college. Started on the beat and worked my way up, and I've never regretted a minute of it. Do have a seat, Jill. Can I get you something to drink?"

"No, thanks. I had a cup of tea at Myrtle's."

"She tells me you're married to a policeman."

"That's right. Jack's a detective in West Chipping. He worked in Washbridge before that."

"Being married to a policeman can't be easy."

"He'd probably say the same thing about being married to me. Myrtle tells me that you're finding retirement a little boring."

"She's right. I am. Weird, isn't it? You spend the last few years counting the days until you can retire, and then once you have, you wonder why you bothered. That's partly why I agreed to talk to you today. Myrtle mentioned that you're working on one of my old cases."

"Do you remember the Kramer case?"

"Of course I do. I remember all the major cases I worked on. My overriding memory of Arnold Kramer is how quiet he was. Like a mouse."

"I haven't had the chance to meet him yet, but that's certainly the impression I get."

"I understand you've been hired by his parents to try to prove his innocence."

"That's right."

"You're going to find that very difficult. The evidence against him was overwhelming: Prior to the murder, Alison's best friend, Karen Little, had seen Kramer threaten Alison. Then, of course, there was the CCTV footage of him at The Burger Barn, handing over the food that would kill Alison. Most damning of all, were the traces of the same poison that were found at Kramer's house."

"How was the poison found? In a routine police search?"

"No. Kramer's housemate's cat died a couple of days after Alison's murder, and it turned out that it had eaten poison. He was the one who reported it to us."

"Were there any other suspects in the case, Walter?"

"None to speak of. As I said before, all the evidence pointed to Kramer."

I stayed with Walter for over an hour. During that time, he talked me through all aspects of the case, and the trial in which Kramer was found guilty by a unanimous verdict. Based on what he'd told me, it was imperative that I speak to Karen Little, Alison's best friend, who had apparently seen Arnold threaten her.

Chapter 11

After I'd finished talking to Walter Staniforth, I met Myrtle at the pub, which was now called The Middle. Myrtle recommended the ploughman's lunch, so we both ordered that.

"What did you make of Walter?" Myrtle said, as she took a sip of wine.

"He was very guarded and defensive, but I suppose that's to be expected."

"In my experience, policemen don't like being second-guessed by private investigators. I think a lot of them are more insecure than they'd care to admit."

"When Jack and I first met, he really had it in for PIs, but that was because of a bad experience he'd had on a case before he moved to Washbridge. He and I used to fight like cat and dog at first."

"Things have obviously improved since then. Do you have children, Jill?"

"Not yet. We both want them, but there's still plenty of time. What about you, Myrtle? Do you have children? Grandchildren?"

"I'm afraid not. Unless you count Hodd and Jobbs." She grinned. "Just between you and me, Jill, I'm actually thinking of upping sticks and moving."

"Leaving Middle Tweaking?"

"Yes. I think the time has come for me to move on."

"But you have such a beautiful home. I'm surprised you can bear to leave the watermill. And this village is idyllic."

"I love the watermill, and I'll miss it terribly. The village too. But I'm not ready to see my time out here."

"You've still got plenty of years ahead of you, Myrtle."

"I hope you're right."

"Where will you go?"

"I've always fancied living on the coast."

"Blackpool? Skegness?"

"Not exactly." She laughed. "I'm on the lookout for a little cottage in a quiet cove. Somewhere I can get up in the morning and look out of the window at the sea. Where I can take early morning walks along a deserted beach."

"You'll be bored to tears, Myrtle."

"Probably, but it's not as though Middle Tweaking is a hive of activity."

"What about Hodd and Jobbs? What was their reaction to your decision?"

"I haven't said anything to them yet, and I'd appreciate it if you didn't either. If nothing comes of it, they need never know. If I do find somewhere, and decide to move, I'll cross that bridge then. Anyway, enough of me. What's your next move on the case you're working on?"

"The victim's best friend gave evidence that my client had made threats against the victim, Alison Reed, after she'd split up with him, so I want to speak to her. I've tried to contact her a few times, but she isn't answering her phone. Hopefully, she'll call me back after she's checked her voicemail. Traces of the poison, which was used to kill Alison, were found at my client's house, so I also want to speak to Arnold's old housemate too."

***

"Come and look at this, Jill." Mrs V walked over to the linen basket and lifted the lid. It was full to the brim.

"I take it your new yarn has arrived?"

"Yes, and it cost me a pretty penny. I do hope this batch doesn't go the way of the last lot."

"I'm sure it won't. Not now that you've sprayed the basket."

In my office, Winky was fast asleep on the sofa. Being the considerate person that I am, I didn't want to wake him, so I tiptoed across the room.

That's when I saw it.

There, on my desk, was the jam jar. The lid was off, and there was no sign of that ugly bug.

"Winky!"

"What?" He jumped up. "Where am I? What day is it?"

"Where's that bug of yours?" I demanded.

"Ivan?" He looked around. "I don't know. In his jam jar, I suppose."

"No, he isn't." I picked up the jar. "Look! The lid's not on."

"Oh?"

"*Oh*? Is that all you can say? Mrs V has just invested a lot of money in a new batch of yarn. If Ivan damages it, you'll be in big trouble."

"If he's already got into the linen basket, it's probably too late. He has a voracious appetite."

Oh bum!

Panic-stricken, I rushed through to the outer office and, without a word to Mrs V, tipped the linen basket over, spilling the contents onto the floor.

"Jill, what are you doing?" Mrs V looked horrified.

"Sorry, but this has to be done." I picked up each ball of wool in turn, to see if I could spot Ivan. Only when I was sure that a ball was Ivan-free, did I put it back into the basket.

Mrs V clearly thought I'd lost my mind, but I persevered until I'd checked every ball of wool. There was no sign of Ivan, thank goodness. The yarn was safe.

"It's okay, Mrs V. Everything's fine."

She gave me the strangest look, as I hurried back into my office where Winky was rolling around on the sofa, laughing his head off.

"What's so funny?"

"Your face when you saw the jam jar was empty." He was in tears now. "It was a picture."

"Never mind that. Start looking for Ivan! If he finds his way back into the linen basket, you'll be in big trouble."

"There's no need. I took him back to Billy the Bugs yesterday."

"You did *what*? I've just spent the last twenty minutes looking for him."

"I know." He laughed even louder. "Priceless."

***

I'd arranged to visit Lori Harty's apartment so that I could see for myself the room from which the painting had been stolen. The apartment block was relatively new and stood on the grounds of what had once been the ice rink. Hence its name: Winter House. An appropriate name given the weather we were experiencing at the moment. Hopefully, Daze and Blaze would apprehend those pesky ice nymphs soon, and it would start to warm up.

Lori's apartment was on the sixth floor. Normally, I would have taken the lift, but I took the stairs because I wanted to get a feel for the exit route that she and her friends had taken when they'd evacuated the building to escape the bees.

Lori had buzzed me into the building, and she was waiting in the doorway of her apartment.

"Come in, Jill. What would you like to see first?"

"Can you show me exactly where the painting was hanging before it disappeared?"

"Yes, of course. Let's go through to the dining room."

It was a sizeable room with a table large enough to seat eight. She stood behind the chair at the far end of the table and pointed at the wall behind me.

"The missing painting was hanging in-between those two."

I had a certain amount of sympathy with Hannah Westbrook's view that less was more. There were an awful lot of paintings in that room, some more attractive than others.

"How big is the painting that disappeared?"

"I'm not very good with measurements."

"How about you compare it to one of those still here? Is it a similar size to any of those?"

She glanced around. "I suppose it would be closest in size to the one above the sideboard. That's why I said there's no way my friends or the pest control man could have taken it out of the building without me seeing it."

"Tell me about the bees. I assume they came in through the patio door?"

"They must have done." She led the way over to the doors, slid one open, and stepped out onto the balcony.

"Do you normally leave this door open when you have a meeting?"

"No, to be honest, that door is rarely open because I

have air conditioning."

"Could it have been open on that particular day?"

"I don't think so."

"Do you normally lock it?"

"Only in the evenings or when I go out. It's just possible that I left it ajar earlier that morning when I went out to water the plants. Or one of the others could have opened it, I suppose. Do you have any theories yet on what happened?"

"Not yet. I suppose it's possible that someone from one of the other apartments could have crept in here after you'd all evacuated."

"I don't see how. When I was at your office, I think I mentioned there are security cameras throughout the building and outside. I had the security man go through the CCTV footage for the period while we were outside, and there was no sign of anyone entering my apartment."

"Right. You said that you went out of the room to make drinks. How long were you gone?"

"Not very long at all. Just long enough to boil a kettle and pour out the drinks. No more than ten minutes."

"And while you were in the kitchen, you heard the bees?"

"That's right, just before I went back through to the dining room, where all hell had broken loose. That's when we all made a run for it."

"Could I take a look outside?"

"Of course. I'll just get my coat."

We took the lift to the ground floor, and I led the way to the front of the building.

"That's your apartment up there, isn't it?" I pointed.

"Yes, the one on the right."

"There's no obvious way for anyone to gain access from the outside. No drainpipes to climb." Just then, I felt something crunch under my foot. "Watch out for the glass, Lori."

"One of the neighbours probably dropped a bottle. They can be so inconsiderate. How difficult would it have been to sweep it up?"

"Do you think I could view the CCTV footage while I'm here?"

"I don't see why not. I'll take you to see Cyril. He's the security guy. Would it be alright if I leave you with him? I need to pop into town to do some shopping."

"Yes, I'll be fine, thanks. I'll let you know as soon as I have something to report."

Cyril showed me the CCTV footage for the day in question, focussing on the period of time when Lori and her friends had evacuated the building. The camera that covered the corridor outside her apartment didn't pick up anyone going inside, from the time of the evacuation until the pest control man arrived. Likewise, after he left, no one entered her apartment until Lori returned.

I thanked Cyril for his help, and then magicked myself over to the town hall in Candlefield, arriving at the subscriptions office with only five minutes to spare. Behind the counter was the same slim young man with the weird quiff.

"I'm back again," I said.

He looked nonplussed, as he clearly didn't remember me from the day before.

"How can I help you, madam?"

"I'd like to renew the subscription on my spell book. It

lapsed a few months ago."

"Certainly." He reached for a form. "Your name, please?"

"Jill Maxwell."

"And the registration number of the spell book?"

I gave him the seven-digit number.

"Including the period when your subscription had lapsed, that will be a total of one hundred and thirty-five pounds, please."

"Thanks." I took out my purse and handed him my credit card.

"What's this, madam?"

"Sorry?"

"I assume you live in the human world."

"That's right. I do. Why?"

"Have you forgotten that credit cards aren't accepted in Candlefield?"

Oh bum! I had.

"Where can I draw out some money?"

"There's a cash machine five minutes from here, near the bus station."

"Okay. Can you hold onto this form until I get back?"

He glanced up at the clock. "I'm very sorry, madam, but we close in two minutes. I'm afraid you'll have to come back tomorrow."

Oh bum, bum, and triple bum!

What would Jack and Ike say when they found out that, once again, I'd failed to renew the subscription, and that Ike would have to stay with us for another day?

***

I'd just arrived home and stepped out of the car when Naomi Normal came hurrying across the road. Oh no! This was unlikely to be good news.

"Jill, do you have a second?" she said.

"Actually Naomi, I was just about to go inside and make dinner."

"It's just that the strangest thing has happened."

"Freddy hasn't gone missing again, has he?"

"No, he's in his cage, but ever since he came back, we keep finding paper clips all around the house. Every time we let him out of his cage, we find a few more. I can't understand it."

"That is strange."

"I can't imagine where they're coming from, Jill."

"Me neither."

"I just thought with you being a private investigator, you might have some bright ideas."

Huh? "No, sorry. Paperclips aren't really my area of expertise."

"Okay, well thanks, anyway."

No wonder I hadn't been able to find a single paper clip all week. Freddy must have nicked them. The little toerag.

I walked up the drive and opened the door, but I couldn't get into the house because the hall was jam-packed full of giant trains and the like. There was a green steam engine, a blue diesel engine, what looked like a passenger carriage, and a signal box.

"Make room for a little one," I shouted.

"Sorry, Jill." Clare, AKA the signal box, moved to one side to allow me in.

"What do you think of our costumes, Jill?" said Jack,

AKA the steam train.

"They're very nice, but there isn't much room in here with the four of you."

"Sorry, Jill," said Tony, AKA the diesel train. "We were just discussing our plans for Sunday. We probably ought to take this discussion outside, guys."

"What do you think of my costume, Jill?" asked Mr Hosey, AKA the railway carriage.

"It's very nice, Mr Hosey, but then you do have a penchant for costumes in your role as neighbourhood watch supervisor. Speaking of which, how is that going at the moment? I haven't spotted you recently, so you must have found some really good camouflage."

"I wish that was true, but actually I've resigned my post."

"From neighbourhood watch? Really? I had no idea."

"I've reached the point where I've exhausted the full range of camouflage outfits, so it's time to pass on the baton to someone else. What about you, Jill, would you be interested?"

"Me? No, I can't do it. There are barely enough hours in the day as it is."

"Come on, guys," Jack said. "Let's go outside and give Jill some room."

It was a tight squeeze, but the two engines, one carriage and the signal box eventually managed to get through the door.

As soon as they'd gone, Ike came running down the stairs.

"Did you do it, Jill? Did you update the subscription?"

"I'm afraid not. Sorry."

His face fell. Or, at least, I think it did. It was hard to tell because it was slowly falling to pieces.

"Why not?"

"I'd totally forgotten that I couldn't use plastic in Candlefield. They insisted on cash."

"Couldn't you have drawn some out?"

"I did, but by then the office had closed. I'll just have to go back there again tomorrow."

He slumped down onto the bottom step. "I told the wife I'd be back tonight."

"I'm really sorry, Ike. I messed up."

"It's okay. This whole thing's my fault. Do you think I could borrow your phone again? I'd better give the wife a call and tell her I'm going to be here for another day."

Chapter 12

When I woke up the next morning, Jack was already out of bed. I figured he must have gone downstairs to get his muesli before Ike made an appearance. I threw on my dressing gown and went down to the kitchen, but there was no sign of him.

How very strange.

If he'd been called into work unexpectedly, he would have left me a note, but there was no sign of one. I went through to the lounge and looked out of the front window; his car was still on the drive.

Where was that man hiding?

I decided to put the kettle on and then I'd go and take another look upstairs for him. The only place he could be was the spare bedroom, but I couldn't believe he'd be playing with his train set while Ike was in there.

I'd just poured the water into the kettle when I happened to glance out of the window. Seated on the bench on the patio, dressed in his big winter coat, was Jack. He had his hood up and his back to me, so he hadn't seen me, and I couldn't see what he was doing. I tapped on the window, but there was no response. I tapped again. Still no response. He clearly couldn't hear me because of his hood.

I threw on a coat, slipped on some shoes and went outside.

"Jack? What are you doing out here?"

When he turned around, I could see that he had a bowl of muesli in his hands.

"And why on earth are you eating muesli in the back garden? It's freezing out here."

"I was worried that Ike might come downstairs while I was in the middle of eating my breakfast. The trouble is the muesli is beginning to freeze over."

"Sometimes you worry me."

"Hello, you two." It was Britt from next door. "Isn't it a bit cold to be having your breakfast out in the garden, Jack?" She grinned.

"Err—I—err—I just fancied some fresh air."

It wasn't surprising that he'd stumbled over his words; he could hardly tell her that he was afraid to eat in the kitchen in case he was joined by our undead houseguest.

Just then, Kit came out to join her. The two of them looked much happier than the last time I'd seen them.

"How are things with you two?" I said, in the hope that a change of subject might stop them from wondering why my crazy husband was sitting in the garden, eating muesli.

"Much better, Jill," Britt said. "I'm sorry we were such misery guts the last time we spoke to you."

"That's okay. I can understand how you'd be disappointed about the marathon."

"We were, but we definitely overreacted. Still, one good thing has come out of it. We've decided that we'd both like a change of career."

"Does that mean you're going to give up the gym and personal training?"

"That's the plan, but we'll be staying in the health sphere. We've talked about it long and hard, and we've decided we'd like to open a small health food restaurant."

"That's very gutsy," Jack said. "Restaurants are a notoriously difficult business to get off the ground."

"We're well aware of that," Kit said. "But we're up for

the challenge, aren't we, darling?"

"Absolutely." Britt gave him a peck on the cheek. "And it's not like we'll be giving up the fitness side entirely. Initially, I intend to carry on with the personal training alongside the restaurant. Hopefully, once it's proven to be a success, I'll go full time and join Kit."

"It sounds like you've given it a lot of thought. I'm sure the two of you will make a success of it." By now, Jack's muesli was completely frozen. "Come on Jack. We'd better get inside."

***

I'd grown very fond of Harold and Ida, the two pigeons who lived on the window ledge outside my office. Even so, I was a little taken aback to find them perched on my desk.

"Hello, you two."

"We're really sorry to impose on you like this, Jill," Harold said. "We wouldn't normally do it, but it was an emergency."

"Why? What's happened?"

"There's a sparrowhawk in the area," Ida said. "If he gets hold of us, we'll be goners."

Winky jumped onto the desk to join them. "That bird is a monster. He's been attacking anything that moves out there. I saw him snatch a pigeon from the building opposite just an hour ago, so I told Harold and Ida they could stay in here until you arrived and sorted it out."

"Until *I* sorted it out? What am I supposed to do? You're the cat. Why don't you sort it out?"

"Are you insane? It's a sparrowhawk! Those things are

psycho; it would tear me to shreds. You'll have to do it, Jill."

"Where is it now?"

Winky jumped off the desk and onto the window ledge. "I can't see it at the moment, but it won't be far away. It keeps swooping in and out."

"Please, Jill," Ida said. "Please help or it'll kill us."

She and Harold looked so scared; how could I refuse? "Don't worry. I'll sort it out."

I walked over to the window, cast a spell to turn myself into a pigeon, and then hopped out onto the ledge. There was no sign of the predator, so I moved gingerly along the narrow ledge until I found a comfortable spot, and then I waited.

A couple of minutes later, a shadow flitted across the building opposite. The sparrowhawk was overhead, and it was diving straight at me.

I would have to time this just right or I'd be the one who was a goner.

When it was just a couple of feet away, I cast another spell to turn myself into a white eagle. The sparrowhawk tried desperately to pull out of the dive, but it was too late, and it crashed into my side, bounced off me, and ended up sprawled on the ledge.

"What happened?" Clearly stunned, it shook its head and looked up at me. "Where did you come from?"

"This is my territory. What are you doing here?"

"I'm really sorry." He managed to stand but he was still rather shaky on his legs. "I had no idea you lived here."

"Well, you do now, don't you?" I lifted one of my talons and waved it in front of his face. "If I were to ask you nicely, do you think you could leave the area?"

"Yes, absolutely. Straight away. You'll never see me on this street again."

"Actually, I'd prefer it if you stayed away from Washbridge altogether."

"No problem. I was thinking of moving somewhere else, anyway."

"Off you trot, then."

He didn't need telling twice. He took to the wing and flew away.

I made my way back inside the office and reverted to my normal appearance.

"That was fantastic, Jill," Ida said.

"Don't mention it. I never did like bullies."

"You make one hot pigeon," Harold said.

"Hey, you, that's quite enough of that!" Ida gave him a gentle slap across the face with her wing.

"Sorry, dear. I don't know what came over me. Thanks very much for helping, Jill."

"No problem."

Harold and Ida were back on the ledge, and Winky was grinning like an idiot.

"What's up with you? What are you grinning at?"

"Harold was right. You do make a hot pigeon."

***

At the time of her death, Alison Reed had been seeing a young man named Kevin Hayes. He'd agreed to talk to me, but he said I would have to meet him at his place of work. He was a barber in Washbridge, at an establishment called Wash Cuts. When I arrived, he was with a customer who, judging by his trousers and beard, was a hipster. When Kevin had finished with his customer, he took me through to the small staff room at the back of the shop.

"I'm sorry I had to ask you to meet me here. I'm engaged now; I live with my fiancée, Josie. She can get very jealous, and she wouldn't appreciate hearing me discuss one of my exes."

"No problem. I appreciate you taking the time to talk to me. As I mentioned on the phone, I've been hired by Arnold Kramer's parents; I'm trying to find evidence to prove that he was wrongly convicted of Alison's murder."

"You do realise that I don't know Arnold, don't you? I've never even met the guy."

"I understand that. It was Alison I wanted to talk to you about. I believe the two of you were an item at the time she was murdered. What did you make of her?"

"I'm not sure I'd call us an *item*. To be perfectly honest, I barely knew her. We'd only been together for just over a week when she was murdered."

"I see. What did you make of her?"

"Not much, really. I suspected she was seeing someone else at the same time as she was supposed to be going out with me."

"Really?"

"Yeah. She was always flirting with other guys. If events hadn't taken the course that they did, I was going to finish with her anyway. She was taking me for a bit of a mug."

"But then she was murdered."

"Yes, and everyone expected me to be grief-stricken. Obviously, I was in shock, but like I said, I barely knew her. When the newspapers and TV interviewed me, I didn't know how to react, and I probably came across as a bit callous."

"What about the police? Did they talk to you?"

"Yes. In fact, for a day or two, I'm pretty sure I was their main suspect. Probably on the basis that I hadn't appeared to be particularly upset when I'd been interviewed on TV. Thankfully, once they arrested Arnold, I didn't hear any more from them."

"Did Alison talk much about Arnold while she was going out with you?"

"Not really. The only thing she said was that her last boyfriend had been a complete loser. She could be quite cruel like that. Very outspoken too; she got herself in trouble a few times when we were out together. If someone looked at her the wrong way, or said something she didn't like, she'd let them know. I found it quite embarrassing, to be honest. That's one of the reasons I was planning to finish with her."

"Do you think it's possible that Alison went to that specific drive-thru, just to taunt Arnold?"

"I doubt it. She was over him. It's more likely she went there because it was the closest to where she lived."

After talking to Kevin, I came away with the impression that Alison was the kind of person who may well have had a number of enemies. She had clearly thought nothing of two-timing her boyfriends, and she was very outspoken. All of that was potentially good news for Arnold because it meant there could be others out there who'd had a reason to want her dead.

Another thought had struck me: How had Arnold

known that Alison would be calling at the drive-thru that night? He must have done to have the poison with him.

I tried Karen Little's number, but there was no answer, so I left a voicemail for her to contact me. Shortly afterwards, I was walking down the high street when my phone rang. I thought it might be Karen, but it was Susan Brown, the woman who had worked alongside Arnold Kramer at the fast food restaurant when the murder took place. She was on maternity leave and had received the message that I wanted to talk to her.

"Thanks for calling me, Susan."

"I understand it's about Arnold Kramer?"

"That's right. If you could spare me just a few minutes sometime, that would be great."

"If it will help Arnold, I'll be happy to. He's such a sweet young man. How does next Monday sound?"

"That works for me. Thanks very much."

***

I magicked myself over to Cuppy C, and was quite surprised to find both Amber and Pearl in the shop. One of their assistants was serving, and the twins were standing to one side of the counter. Judging by the way both of them were gesticulating, they were having a heated discussion.

"Hey, you two. How come you're both in here today? Are the little ones upstairs in the creche?"

"No. Mum's taken them out for the day," Pearl said. "Lester's got the day off from the fish man, so they decided to go out for a picnic, seeing as it was such a lovely day."

"Think yourselves lucky. It's freezing in Washbridge. What were you two arguing about when I came in?"

"Will you please tell Amber she's wrong?" Pearl said.

"No, I'm not," Amber objected. "You're the one who's wrong."

"If you want me to adjudicate, you're going to have to tell me what you're talking about. Maybe then I can offer an opinion."

"Pearl thinks she's taller than me," Amber said. "And that's clearly nonsense. I'm at least half an inch taller than she is."

"In your dreams." Pearl laughed. "I'm three quarters of an inch taller than you, at least."

"Come on, Jill," Amber said. "Tell her that I'm the tallest."

"Actually, I would say you're both exactly the same height."

"Nonsense." Amber stood right next to Pearl and put her hand first on her head and then on Pearl's. "See, I'm the tallest."

"You're standing on tiptoe!" Pearl said.

"No, I'm not. And anyway, your heels are higher than mine."

"Girls, girls." I held up my hand to silence them. "I can see this argument is likely to run and run, so I'm going to get a drink."

"It's alright, Jill," Pearl said. "We were just going back to the counter, anyway. What would you like? A caramel latte?"

"To tell you the truth, I rather fancy a banana milkshake."

"You never drink milkshakes."

"Well, I fancy one today."

"And a blueberry muffin?" Amber said.

"Actually, I'd like a gingerbread man."

They exchanged a glance.

"Are you sure you're the real Jill Maxwell?" Amber said.

"I'm allowed to have something different every now and then, aren't I? Sheesh! What's with the third degree?"

While Pearl got my milkshake and gingerbread, Amber said, "You haven't heard our latest news yet, have you?"

"Yes, I have. You told me the other day. You're going to close down the cake shop."

"Not that. That's old news."

"What's the *new* news then?"

"Actually, we have good and bad news, and good news."

"So, three lots of news?"

"No, just two. One of them is good *and* bad."

"You'd better tell me that one first."

"The good news is that Jemima is having a baby."

"That's great. She'll make a great mum."

"I agree, but it's also bad because it rather leaves us in the lurch."

"Will she be coming back after she's had the baby?"

"She hasn't made her mind up yet, but either way, we need to find someone in the short-term. How about you? Do you fancy working in the creche, Jill?"

"Me? Are you joking?"

"Mum said you were a natural."

Pearl handed me the milkshake. "Yeah, she said that when her neighbours came around, you were the only one who could get the baby to stop crying."

"That was sheer fluke. So, what's the other good news?"

"You'll never guess who's been nominated for the Candlefield Businesswoman of the Year award."

"I have no idea. Is it anyone I know?"

"Yes. Me," Amber said.

"And me," Pearl said.

"Both of you?"

"Yes. It's actually a joint nomination."

I laughed; I couldn't help myself.

"It's not funny, Jill. It's a very prestigious honour, and we're confident that we'll win."

Chapter 13

I was still chuckling to myself when I arrived back at my office building. Seriously, how had Amber and Pearl been nominated for Candlefield Businesswoman of the Year? It had to be some kind of wind-up. I love those two girls to bits, but some of the ideas they came up with for Cuppy C were insane. Now, if someone had nominated me as businesswoman of the year, I could have understood that. After all, I did epitomise entrepreneurship.

When I walked into the outer office, Mrs V was on the phone. The moment she spotted me, she began to act rather suspiciously. She swivelled around on her chair, so she had her back to me, and began to speak in a very low voice, so that I couldn't hear what she was saying. I was intrigued, but I couldn't very well hang around eavesdropping so I left her to it.

"Well, well, well, if it isn't pigeon girl," Winky said.

"I take it that's your new name for me?"

"You should embrace it. It makes you sound like a superhero."

"I don't think so."

"What's the old bag lady up to out there?"

"What do you mean?"

"That's the third call she's taken today."

"So? That's what she's there for, to answer the phone."

"Yes, but usually I can hear every word she says. She's deliberately been speaking much quieter than usual. I've not been able to hear a word she's said."

"You shouldn't be listening in on her calls. They're

private."

"If you ask me, there's something going on, and you need to find out what it is. Ask her what she's up to."

"I will not. Unlike you, Winky, I have better things to do with my time than intrude on other people's affairs."

"Don't give me that." He scoffed. "You're the nosiest person I know."

"How dare you! That's an outrageous thing to say."

Just then, the temperature in the office dropped dramatically, and Winky shot under the sofa. Moments later, the colonel and Priscilla materialised.

"Good day, Jill," the colonel said.

"Hello, Colonel. Priscilla. You two are looking very chipper."

"We're on top of the world, aren't we, Cilla?"

"We are, Briggsy." She beamed. "Why don't you tell Jill our news?"

"I think you should be the one to tell her, Cilla."

"Come on, you two. One of you had better tell me. You can't leave me hanging like this."

In the end, it was the colonel who took the lead. "The thing is, Jill, Cilla and I have decided that we need a complete change. Something that will blow away the cobwebs."

"What kind of change?"

"We've decided to sell the business."

"Hauntings Unlimited? I thought you'd just turned it around, and that it was doing really well now."

"It is, which is precisely why it's the right time to sell. According to my research, we should make a handsome profit, which we'll use to finance our next little adventure."

"Which is?"

"We're going on a cruise ship."

"Very nice, but do you really need to sell the business just to pay for a holiday?"

"It's not a holiday," the colonel said. "We're going to make the cruise ship our permanent home."

"You're going to live on a cruise ship?"

"That's right. For the foreseeable future, at least."

"Does that mean you'll be haunting the ship?"

"Essentially, yes."

"Sun and sea? That does sound appealing. When will you be going?"

"We've not finalised our plans yet. We'll need to sell the business first, and there's Terry Salmon to consider."

"Terry? You've met with him, then?"

"Yes. I'm showing him the ropes, so to speak. He's a quick learner, so it shouldn't take very long."

"That's good to hear. When I saw him in GT, he seemed very nervous and unsure of himself."

"That's not unusual; newbies usually are. Terry will be fine by the time Cilla and I have sold the business and moved to the cruise ship. I hope you'll forgive me for saying this, Jill, but you're looking a little tired these days. You work way too hard. You and your husband should treat yourself to a long break. You should take a cruise, and we could all meet up for drinks."

"It's a nice thought, Colonel, but we don't have cruise-type money. We'll be lucky if we can afford a weekend in Filey this year."

"I'm really sorry to hear that, Jill. I do hope things turn around for you soon. Anyway, we must get going. We just wanted to tell you our good news."

"Don't forget to say goodbye before you leave for your new life on the high seas."

***

Curiously, there was only one male member of WFAAS. I really shouldn't have been surprised because most of the men I knew were philistines.

The gentleman in question was a Mr Finley McAdams, and I'd arranged to meet him at his house, which was on the outskirts of West Chipping. The detached property, which was a quarter of a mile away from the next house, had a picture-perfect front garden.

I pulled the ornate metal chain, and a bell rang somewhere deep inside the house. Moments later, a petite woman in her sixties came to the door and handed me a white plastic bag, which was bursting at the seams and quite heavy.

"There are some nice shoes in there," she said. "I've only worn them once because they're too narrow."

She was just about to close the door when I said, "Just a minute. I think there may have been a mistake."

"You do take shoes, don't you? The leaflet said you accepted clothes *and* shoes."

"I think you must have mistaken me for someone else. I'm not here to collect this."

"Aren't you from Washbridge Senior Support?"

"No, sorry."

"I do beg your pardon." She took the bag back. "Who are you, then?"

"My name's Jill Maxwell. I'm here to see Mr Finley McAdams."

"Are you the private investigator lady?"

"That's me."

"I do apologise for the confusion. I'm Barbara. Finley is my husband. You'd better come in."

I stepped inside, onto a thick pile carpet that looked and smelled brand new. "Would you like me to take off my shoes?" I offered.

"No, dear, that won't be necessary. Finley is out the back; in the shed. He spends more time in there than he does in the house. Not that I'm complaining because it allows me to watch my TV in peace."

She led me through to the kitchen, opened the back door and pointed to the shed, which was halfway down the garden.

As I neared the shed, I heard a strange noise coming from inside. Mr McAdams was obviously working on something. I knocked on the door, but he didn't hear me. I tried again with the same result, so I opened the door slowly and stepped inside.

Mr McAdams was wearing a safety visor, and he had a small electric saw in his hand. He must have seen the door open because he switched off the power tool and nodded a greeting.

"Hello, young lady. Are you the private investigator?"

"That's right. Jill Maxwell."

"I'm awfully sorry I wasn't in the house to greet you. I completely lost track of time. I've been so very busy."

"No problem."

"Do you mind if we talk in here? If we go into the house, I'll have to get changed because the wife doesn't appreciate me wandering around in there with my overalls on."

"In here will be fine."

"You said your name was Jill, didn't you?"

"That's right. Jill Maxwell."

"Tell me, Jill, do you have any leads yet?"

"Not yet, but then so far, I've only spoken to Lori and Hannah."

"How can I be of assistance?"

"Perhaps you could start by talking me through the events of the last meeting of the art appreciation society?"

"Yes, of course."

The story he told pretty much matched the one I'd heard from Hannah Westbrook: how they'd met in Lori's dining room, chatted for a while, and then Lori had gone through to the kitchen to make drinks.

"That's when the bees appeared," he said. "And we had to evacuate the apartment."

"Did you see how the bees got in, Mr McAdams?"

"No, but I assume they must have come in through the patio door. One minute they weren't there, and the next, we were overrun with them. I was lucky to get out without being stung. I believe poor Hannah took one on the way out."

"She did, yes. Tell me, Mr McAdams, what do you think of the painting that was stolen?"

"It's a nice piece; there's no doubt about that, but to be perfectly honest with you, I think Lori paid well over the odds for it. I don't know where she got that kind of money from because she's always pleading poverty to me."

"Did you notice anything suspicious on your way into the building that day?"

"Nothing at all, but then it's always very quiet there."

"Can you think of anyone who might have taken the painting?"

"Not really. I mean, it's not like it's a Turner or anything. I did have one thought, but I probably should keep it to myself."

"Please tell me. It might help."

"Do you promise it will stay between us?"

"Of course."

"My first thought when I heard the painting had gone missing was that Lori must have overstretched herself financially, and decided to go after the insurance money."

"Are you suggesting that she might have staged the theft?"

"Yes. No. Probably not. That's just the first thing that popped into my head. Take no notice of me. What do I know?"

When we'd finished our little chat, he led me back to the house where his wife was waiting to meet me. She walked me through the house and saw me out.

"Was Finley able to assist you, dear?"

"Yes, he was very helpful."

"I don't really know what he sees in those meetings. I sometimes think he only goes there for the other ladies."

I was determined not to go home without having first renewed my subscription for the spell book.

I magicked myself over to the Candlefield town hall in plenty of time to ensure that I didn't fall foul of the three-thirty deadline. Once again, the same slim young man with the strange quiff was behind the counter. And, once again, he clearly didn't remember me.

"How can I help you, madam?"

"I'd like to renew the subscription for my spell book. I inadvertently allowed it to lapse a few months ago."

"Certainly, madam. We'll just need to complete this form. Your name, please?"

"Jill Maxwell."

I gave him the registration number of the book and handed over the cash.

"That's everything I need. I'll just update our records." He tapped away on the keyboard for a few minutes. "All done. Everything's up to date."

"Great. Does that mean I'll be able to update my spell book when I get back home?"

"You will. Just follow the instructions on the back page and it should update immediately."

"Excellent. Thank you very much."

Ike and Jack would be delighted that I'd finally managed to renew my subscription. As soon as I got home, I'd update the book, find the spell I needed, and put Ike out of his misery. He'd be able to go home to his wife, and Jack and I would be able to enjoy our evening meal without having to share the table with the undead.

***

As soon as I walked through the door, Ike came running downstairs.

"Jill, please tell me you managed to renew your subscription."

"I certainly did. I'm just about to go and update the spell book."

"That's great news. I can't wait to get back home to the

missus."

"Why don't you go upstairs and—err—freshen up? I'll do the update then come and find you."

"Will do, Jill." He shot back up the stairs.

I went through to the lounge, took out the spell book, and followed the instructions to perform the update. This time, thankfully, it processed without a hitch. After a few moments, a message appeared at the bottom of the page, to confirm that the book was now up to date. I consulted the index for the spell I needed to reverse Ike's condition. For one horrible moment, I thought it wasn't there because there was nothing listed under 'Z'. Then I spotted it under 'P' with the catchy title of Pseudo Zombie. If I'd had more time, I would have submitted a suggestion that they cross-reference it under 'Z' as Zombie, Pseudo, but I had more important matters to attend to.

I flicked to the page where it was supposed to be listed, but all I found was a heading; there were no detailed instructions on how to perform the spell. Instead, there was just a short note, which said that particular spell was part of the premium package.

Premium package? What *premium package*? I'd never seen any mention of that in the spell book before.

I checked the front of the book and found a note confirming that in this latest edition, certain spells were now available only to those who had paid for the premium package upgrade. And when I read on, my heart sank.

To upgrade to the premium package, please make the additional payment at the subscriptions office in Candlefield town hall, which is open Monday to Friday, from 9:30 to 3:30.

Oh, bum! This nightmare was never-ending.

I went through to the hallway, and shouted, "Ike, you'd better come down here. I'm afraid I've got some bad news for you."

***

I was in the kitchen when Jack arrived home from work.

"Has Ike gone?" he said. "Do we have the house to ourselves now?"

"No. He's still upstairs in the spare bedroom."

"What? Don't tell me you forgot to go to the subscriptions office, Jill."

"No, I didn't forget."

"Did you forget to take the money with you?"

"No, I didn't forget that either."

"How come you still can't reverse the spell, then?"

"Because apparently, in the latest edition of the book there are now two types of spells: standard and premium. Unless you pay extra for the premium package, you can't access the premium ones."

"And don't tell me. The spell you need is one of the premium ones?"

"Correct. I'll have to go back to the subscriptions office on Monday, to pay for the premium package."

"What I don't understand is why, if you're the most powerful witch in Candlefield, you can't come up with the spell yourself?"

"Because, Jack, it isn't as simple as all that. I can conjure up most spells, but this one is very unusual. Turning someone into a pseudo-zombie is not something that has ever been done before and it's very tricky. I wouldn't know where to begin. I asked Grandma, and even she didn't have a clue how to do it. We're just going to have to wait until I've purchased the premium package on Monday. Until then, we're stuck with Ike."

I'd taken Ike's dinner up to the spare bedroom. He was quite understanding when I'd explained that we'd prefer to eat alone, and that it was nothing personal. Back downstairs, Jack and I were enjoying the roast chicken dinner that he'd prepared.

"By the way, I called in at the corner shop on the way home," he said.

"Did you see the giant fan he's had installed?"

"I did. It looks like a wind tunnel behind that screen. But, to be honest, that was the least of Little Jack's problems."

"How come?"

"When I left, he had a queue of irate customers. They'd all returned their baskets, but they hadn't been refunded their pound."

Chapter 14

It was Saturday morning and, even though it was still freezing outside, Jack was full of the joys of spring.

"Today is going to be fantastic Jill," he gushed.

"Hmm, for you maybe. You get to go go-karting while I'm stuck in the house with Ike."

"Don't be so melodramatic. You don't have to stay in. You can do whatever you like. And, don't forget we've got the fancy dress party to look forward to, tonight."

"Whoop-di-doo. It just gets better and better."

"Come on, Jill, you know you'll enjoy it when you get there."

"Couldn't we just give it a miss? We could stay in tonight."

"And do what? Watch TV?"

"It wasn't TV I had in mind." I flashed him my super-sexy smile.

"With Ike in the next room? I don't think so. Anyway, we promised we'd go to the fancy dress do, and as the band's star soloist, everyone will expect you to be there. Are you still planning on wearing the witch's outfit?"

"Yeah. I don't see the point in spending good money to hire a costume when I can wear that for nothing. I managed to get hold of one of the green ones."

"Why don't you go and put it on now? You know how sexy I think you look in those."

"I'd love to, but like you just said, Ike's upstairs."

"Spoilsport."

"You're the spoilsport. You won't even tell me what your costume is."

"I want it to be a surprise."

"It had better be good after all this build up. Has Ike been downstairs yet?"

"Yeah, he came down earlier to get some corn flakes. I was eating my muesli at the time, and I thought for a horrible moment that he was going to join me, but he took his breakfast upstairs."

"What time is Peter coming?"

"He should be here any minute now. I'd better go and look out for him." Jack walked through to the lounge and I followed. "The weather is getting worse out there." He pointed. "Look, the cars are frozen over. It should never be as cold as that at this time of year."

"I told you why that is. It's the ice nymphs."

"What did they do to make it so cold?"

"I don't know. The only reason I know they're responsible is because Daze told me."

"Pete's here." Jack gave me a quick peck on the lips and then hurried out of the door.

Waiting for him in the car were Peter and Mikey who both gave me a wave. As soon as Jack had joined them, they drove away.

What was I going to do with myself all day? Before I could even begin to think about it, I needed coffee to wake me up. I'd just switched on the kettle when I heard the familiar uneven clomping sound on the stairs; Ike was on his way down.

He looked even worse than he had the day before.

"Morning, Jill," he said.

"Morning. You're looking rough today, Ike."

"Is that supposed to be a joke?"

"No, sorry. I just meant—err—never mind. Would you like a coffee?"

"Yes, please."

We were both seated at the kitchen table when I heard the door open. Had Jack forgotten something?

"It's only me," Kathy shouted.

Oh bum!

"Ike, stay here and don't make a sound."

I hurried out of the kitchen, closing the door behind me.

"Hi there," I said, trying not to freak out at the thought of the pseudo-zombie in my kitchen. "I wasn't expecting to see you today. I told Jack I thought you'd be working."

"May said she could manage the shop by herself just for one day."

"What about Lizzie? Where is she?"

"Gone to a friend's house for the day. The girl's mother is going to take them to the cinema this afternoon, so I thought you and I might do something."

"What did you have in mind? Do you want to go into Washbridge and take a look around the shops?"

"No, I have a much better idea."

Kathy shared her idea with me, and although it definitely wasn't what I'd been expecting, I did like the sound of it.

"Sure, I'd be up for that."

"Great! But I need a drink first."

Before I could stop her, Kathy had walked through to the kitchen.

Oh bum! How would I explain away the undead seated at the table?

"Did you know I was coming?" Kathy shouted.

"No. I told you; I thought you were working."

"So, how come there are two cups of coffee on the

table?"

"Err, I was feeling really thirsty, so I made myself two cups."

"You are seriously weird, Jill. Is it okay if I have one of these?"

"Sure." I joined her at the kitchen table. There was no sign of Ike, and I couldn't figure out where he'd gone.

"It's cold in here," Kathy said. "Do you mind if I shut the window?"

"Go ahead." It was only then that I realised that Ike must have climbed out into the back garden and been unable to shut the window properly from the outside. Poor thing. He had to be freezing out there. If he wasn't careful, even more bits of him would drop off.

***

I'm not sure which one of them was more surprised to see us: Jack and Peter were both standing there, open-mouthed. Mikey was too busy trying on his crash helmet to even notice us.

"What are you two doing here?" Peter asked.

"We thought we'd show you boys how it's done," Kathy said.

"In your dreams." Peter laughed.

"Did you know you were going to come here, Jill?" Jack said.

"No, honestly. I was just having a cup of coffee when Kathy turned up. It was her idea."

"You do realise that these are not pedal-karts, don't you?" Peter said. "They have real engines."

"Don't be so patronising, Pete," Kathy snapped. "Jill

and I can take you two, any day of the week."

Jack and Peter exchanged a look.

"That sounds like a challenge to me," Jack said.

"It certainly does." Peter turned to us. "If you two are so confident, why don't we make it a competition, men versus women?"

"What about Mikey?" Kathy said.

"He'll be neutral. For the purposes of the competition, it'll be Jack and me versus you and Jill. Whoever comes in first between the four of us takes the race. Agreed?"

"Fine by us," Kathy said. "This is going to be easy money."

"Who mentioned money?" Jack said.

"We should have a small wager to make it interesting." Kathy was surprisingly confident. "What do you reckon, Jill?"

"Definitely. Why don't we say whichever team loses has to pay for everything today?"

"You're on." Peter clearly liked the idea.

"What about you, Jack?" I said. "Are you up for it?"

"Definitely. Bring it on!"

While Peter, Jack, and Mikey were choosing their karts, Kathy and I went to the counter. The geeky, spotty young man on duty, gave us each some leathers to go over our own clothes, and a crash helmet.

"These smell." I held the leathers at arm's length. "Don't you have any newer ones?"

"Sorry, lady. All of them are like that. It's an adrenaline-packed sport."

"Come on, Jill. Hurry up." Kathy had already put on her leathers. "We don't want to miss the first race."

Reluctantly, I slipped on the smelly leathers, which were at least two sizes too big for me, then we climbed into the two remaining go-karts.

As we waited for the race to begin, Kathy turned to me. "We have to win this, Jill, or we'll never hear the end of it."

"Don't worry. It's in the bag."

"Are you okay, Mikey?" Kathy shouted.

He looked really excited and gave her the thumbs up.

The oval track was bordered by walls of tyres, which looked like they'd seen their fair share of crashes. Once we were all lined up on what passed for the grid, the guy in charge stepped forward and raised his arm.

"Three, two, one. Go!"

We were off. Peter nosed ahead of Jack; behind him was Mikey. Next came Kathy, and I was bringing up the rear. The track was very narrow, so there were very few opportunities to overtake. With three laps to go, Jack was in the lead, Mikey was second, Peter third, then came Kathy. I was still in last place. One of the two guys looked certain to take this race, which meant that if we were to have any chance, we'd have to do much better in the next one.

But then, as we approached the penultimate bend, Kathy floored the throttle and overtook Peter and Mikey on the inside. Jack glanced nervously over his shoulder as he sensed her gaining on him. At the final bend, Jack went a little too wide, and Kathy took her chance to overtake him on the inside.

As she took the chequered flag, she punched the air.

"First race to us," she shouted, as we all climbed out of

the karts.

"You forced me off the track, Kathy," Peter protested.

"Stop whinging." She laughed. "All's fair in love and go-karting."

There was a ten-minute break before the start of the next race. Peter, Mikey, and Jack were huddled together at one table. Kathy and I were at another.

"You can't pull any more manoeuvres like that, Kathy," I said. "You could get hurt."

"Don't be silly. It was perfectly safe. No way am I letting those two win."

I got a much better start in the next race; I was in second place behind Mikey. I had no idea how the others were doing, and I certainly had no intention of looking back. Mikey had really got the hang of it, and he seemed to be improving on every lap.

On the penultimate lap, Jack overtook me on the inside. If I didn't retake the lead, the guys would level the match. I tried to overtake him on the next bend, but he held the corner and I couldn't get through. The same thing happened on the final bend. The race finished with Jack in first place, Mikey second, and me in third. Peter was next, and Kathy came in last.

"One race apiece," Jack said, triumphantly. "Next one will be the decider."

"Sorry, Kathy," I said. "I thought I had that one sewn up."

"Don't worry about it. As long as we win the next race, it's all good."

At the start of the third and final race, Kathy and Peter

shot out in front. The lead seemed to change hands on almost every lap. Mikey was in third place, and Jack and I were in joint last position, which meant we were pretty much out of the race.

The competition looked set to be decided between Peter and Kathy. As they reached the next bend, Peter tried to overtake her, but she refused to give way. Their wheels touched and both karts spun off the course and into the wall of tyres. That meant Mikey was now in first place. More importantly, whoever finished in second place, between Jack and me, would ensure their team took the overall competition. Seeing his opportunity, Jack hit the throttle, and raced ahead of me. There was only one lap to go, and no way that I could allow him to win.

He was on the final straight when, suddenly, his car ground to a halt. I shot past him and took the chequered flag behind Mikey.

Kathy and I were out of our karts, hugging one another and dancing around like big kids, celebrating our win.

"What happened there, mate?" Peter said.

"I've no idea." Jack shook his head. "It just stopped." He'd called over the man in charge who was now looking over the stricken vehicle. "What's wrong with it?"

"Looks like you ran out of fuel. You must've been giving it too much throttle."

"Surely, there should be enough fuel to get through the race."

"There is. More than enough. To be honest, I've never seen this happen before. You must have really been hammering it."

Back outside, Kathy and I were in jubilant mood; Jack

and Peter looked despondent.

"Did you enjoy yourself, Mikey?" I asked.

"It was fantastic, Auntie Jill. Can I come again, Mum?"

"Of course you can," Kathy said.

"You've changed your tune." Peter rolled his eyes. "You were the one who said you didn't want him to go go-karting."

"Yes, but now I've seen how competent he is, I'm okay with it. And besides, it's fun. We enjoyed it, didn't we, Jill?"

"We sure did."

Kathy, Peter, and Mikey went home in their car, while Jack and I took mine.

"You're very quiet, Jack."

"You cheated," he snapped.

"You're just a bad loser."

"There's no way that go-kart ran out of petrol. You must have used magic on it."

"Don't be ridiculous." I laughed. "We won fair and square."

Snigger.

When we arrived home, Ike appeared from behind the house. There was an icicle hanging from what was left of his nose.

"Are you okay, Ike?" Jack asked.

"No, I'm freezing. Someone shut the window and locked me out of the house."

Oh bum! I'd forgotten all about poor old Ike.

"Come inside." I felt terrible. "I'll make you a warm drink."

***

Jack and I had a light dinner because we knew there would be food at the fancy dress do. He was still sulking because Kathy and I had beaten them at go-karting. I was pretty sure he still suspected me of using magic, which of course I had, but there was no way I was ever going to admit it.

"I think I'll go upstairs and put my costume on," I said, after we finished eating. "Do I get to see yours now?"

Before he could answer, his phone rang.

"Jack Maxwell speaking. What? Isn't there anyone else? Okay, I'll be there as soon as I can."

"What was that all about?" I asked.

"There's an emergency. I have to go into work."

"Right now?"

"Yeah. Two or three people are off with a stomach bug, so I have no choice."

"How long will you be there?"

"I've no idea, but from the sound of it, it could be all night."

"Never mind." I sighed. "I'll just stay in and watch TV."

"You can't do that; everyone is expecting us. If you go, you can explain that I've been called into work."

"I don't want to go there by myself."

"Come on, Jill. You're the star of the band. You have to at least make an appearance. You needn't stay long—just an hour or so, then you can sneak away."

"Okay, if I must."

Jack had left, and I'd changed into my green witch's

costume. I was just about to leave when Ike called to me from upstairs, "Jill, hold on."

"What is it? I'm just on my way out."

"I don't suppose I could come with you, could I?"

"To the fancy dress do?"

"Yeah. I mean, who would know? They'll all think I'm Jack."

"I'm really not sure that's a good idea."

"Please, Jill, just for an hour. I've been locked out of the house all day. I need something to cheer me up."

How could I refuse when I felt at least partly responsible for him being stuck outside in the freezing cold? "Okay, but whatever you do, you mustn't speak to anyone, or they'll realise you're not Jack."

"Don't worry, I won't say a word."

So it was that I found myself walking down the street, dressed in a green witch's costume, accompanied by a pseudo-zombie.

Mr Hosey, dressed as a stick of rock, was on the door of the scout hut.

"I like your outfit, Jill. Wow, Jack, you look spectacular."

Ike nodded his head but said nothing.

Once inside, we both headed straight for the refreshments. Ike was clearly ravenous, and he began to devour the sausage rolls and crisps. Because part of his mouth was missing, he was making an awful mess; crumbs were going everywhere.

"You can't let people see you eating like that, Ike," I said. "Come on. Let's find a quiet spot somewhere."

Tucked away at one end of the room, I figured we'd be

safe, but then the Normals came over to talk to us. They appeared to be dressed as alphorns.

"Hi, Jill. I really like your outfit," Naomi said.

"Look at Jack's costume," Norm said. "Where did you get that from, Jack?"

Ike said nothing.

"Sorry, he can't talk," I said. "He wants to stay in character and zombies don't speak."

"Of course. I understand."

I figured I'd been there long enough, and I was ready to go home, but I couldn't leave without Ike, and he'd wandered off somewhere.

I spotted him near to the door, so I hurried over, but before I could drag him outside, Britt and Kit appeared. Britt was dressed as a fairy and Kit had chosen a gorilla costume.

"Hi, Jill," Britt said. "I love your green witch's outfit."

"Thanks."

"Who's your ugly friend? Is that Jack?" Before I could stop him, Kit had reached out to touch Ike's face.

This was a disaster. Any moment now, Ike's head would fall off, and how would I explain that?

"Do you like it?" Jack said, removing the zombie head.

I stared at him in disbelief.

"It's really great, Jack," Britt said. "If there was a prize for the best costume, you'd definitely win it."

Kit and Britt headed over to the refreshments, leaving me, still open-mouthed, staring at Jack.

"You? How?" I couldn't find the words.

"What do you think? I got this from the fancy dress shop your friends work at."

"I thought you were Ike."

"Why would you think that?"

"Because when you couldn't make it, he came with me instead. How come you're back, anyway?"

"I was halfway there when I got a phone call to say I wasn't needed. Hang on, did you say Ike came here with you?"

"Yeah."

"Where is he now?"

"I don't know. We'd better find him and quick."

"You take that side, and I'll take this one," Jack said. "When one of us finds him, send the other a text. Okay?"

"Okay."

I was pretty sure I knew where Ike would be, so I headed straight for the snacks. Sure enough, he was helping himself to cocktail sausages. I was just about to grab him by the arm and drag him away when it occurred to me that I might actually pull his arm off.

"Ike!"

"Hey, Jill. I didn't know where you'd gone, so I thought I'd—"

"Come on. We have to leave right now."

"But I was just going to get some crisps."

"No time. Sorry." I sent Jack a quick message. *"Found him. Meet us outside."*

Five minutes later, the three of us were on our way home.

"That was too close for comfort," Jack said. "And I didn't even manage to get anything to eat."

"You can have one of these." Ike offered him one of the cocktail sausages he'd managed to grab before I made him leave.

Jack looked at them in Ike's flaky hands and declined.

"Jack?" Mr Hosey appeared out of nowhere and glanced back and forth between the two zombies. "How come there are two of you?"

"I—err—can explain," Jack spluttered. "It—err—"

I didn't have time for this, so I quickly cast the 'forget' spell, and the three of us made our escape.

Chapter 15

It was Monday morning and Jack had spent the last fifteen minutes regaling me with stories of his TrainCon experience.

"It was hilarious, Jill." He laughed. "The diesel engines and steam engines were really going at it."

"That's the bit I don't understand. If they were all wearing train costumes, how exactly did they manage to fight?"

"They weren't exactly fighting. They were just kind of bumping into one another, but it was so funny."

"It sounds it. Makes me almost wish I'd been there." Not. "By the way, you've not forgotten that we're having dinner with Luther and Rebecca tonight, have you?"

"Is that still on? I thought the ruby fairies were coming tonight?"

"They'll be here at six o'clock. All we have to do is pop them into the airing cupboard, and then we'll be good to go. We're not seeing Luther until eight."

"I'm looking forward to meeting Rebecca. Don't you find it rather weird that Luther is going out with a werewolf, but he has absolutely no idea?"

"Not really. When you meet Rebecca, you'll see that she looks just like a female human. She's very pretty."

"Yes, but she can turn herself into a wolf."

"Really? Who knew that's what werewolves do?"

"You know what I mean."

"It's not like Luther is the only human who's in a relationship with a sup but isn't aware of it. In fact, as I recall, there was a time not so long ago that you fell into that very category."

"That was different. You're a witch, and witches are almost human. It would have been different if you'd been a vampire or a werewolf. I would have known then."

"Do you honestly believe that?"

"Definitely. There's no doubt in my mind about it."

I was just on my way out of the door when I heard a clump, clump, clump on the stairs behind me.

It could only be one person (creature?).

"Jill, you won't forget you have to upgrade your subscription today, will you?" Ike said.

"Don't worry, it's on my list of things to do. You can rest assured that by tonight you should be able to go home."

"Thanks, Jill. I can't wait to see the missus again."

***

As I had skipped breakfast, I called in at Coffee Games to get a coffee to-go. Thankfully, it was a game-free day, so I wasn't forced to put up with one of those ridiculous parlour games.

I'd got my coffee and was just about to leave when, out of the corner of my eye, I spotted Mrs V sitting at a table near the window. I was just about to go over and say hello when I realised that she wasn't alone; sitting opposite her was a young man. The two of them appeared to be studying some paperwork on the table in front of them, so I figured I shouldn't intrude.

***

There was a white envelope on my desk addressed to the business owner. The letter was on a Washbridge City Council letterhead and read:

Notice of new signage regulations.
To whom it may concern.
This is to inform you that new signage regulations have been introduced. This will affect all business owners who have signs on the exterior of their buildings.
With immediate effect, the council have decided that all signage in the city must be of the format:
Text colour: Navy Blue
Background: White
Any signs that do not conform to the new standard must be replaced within twenty-one days from the date of this letter, or a fixed fine of one hundred pounds will be levied. Additional fines (of one hundred pounds) will be levied on the first day of each month until such time as the sign has been replaced.

"What?" I yelled. "How can they do this? It's outrageous. This is going to cost the businesspeople of Washbridge a small fortune. How do they expect us to ever make a profit?"

"Is something the matter?" Winky, who was sitting on the sofa, looked up from his magazine.

"Yes, something is most definitely the matter. This is bureaucracy gone mad. They're trying to tell us what colour our signs have to be."

"Who are 'they'?"

"The city council. According to this letter, unless I replace my sign, they're going to fine me every month."

"That doesn't seem fair."

"It's not fair, and I intend to tell them precisely that. I'm not going to take this sitting down."

"Good for you."

I stormed out of my office.

"Are you okay, Jill?" Mrs V said. "I thought I heard you shouting?"

"No, I'm not okay." I told her about the city council's unreasonable demands.

"That does sound a little unfair."

"It's more than a *little* unfair. It's an outrage. By the way, I saw you in Coffee Games earlier."

"Did you, dear?" I thought she might tell me who the man was that I'd seen her with, or what they'd been up to, but she quickly changed the subject. "Don't go getting into trouble at the city council."

"Don't worry. I won't."

***

I was spitting feathers all the way to Washbridge City Council offices. The woman behind the desk in reception was wearing a smart blue uniform. According to the badge on her lapel, her name was Imelda.

"Good morning, Imelda. Could you please point me in the direction of the department that deals with signage?"

"Sorry, I'm not sure what you mean."

"I want to speak to someone in whichever department is responsible for signage in Washbridge."

"Do you mean the council's own signs?"

"No, I mean the signs that are displayed by local businesses. I've just received a letter informing me that new regulations have been introduced governing those signs."

"Do you have the letter with you?"

"No, I'm afraid I left it on the desk in my office."

"Okay. If you could just wait there for a moment, I'll see what I can find out."

She made a couple of phone calls.

"It appears that the Works Department deal with all matters relating to signage. The man in charge is a Mr Arthur Carter."

"In that case, can I make an appointment to see Mr Carter?"

"Actually, I've just spoken to him, and he said he'd be happy to spend a few minutes with you now."

"Excellent. Where do I find him?"

"He's on the fifth floor; in room 512."

"Thanks. Where are the lifts?"

"They're over there on the right, but I'm afraid they're both out of order. We're waiting for the maintenance man to come. The stairs are to your left."

"Right, thanks."

By the time I'd reached the fifth floor, I was struggling to catch my breath. I knocked on the door of room 512, and a female voice shouted, "Come in."

The young woman behind the desk had short punk-like hair. "Are you the lady to see Mr Carter?"

"That's right. About the signage."

"He's through that door over there. You can go straight in."

Carter, a rotund, middle-aged man with a moustache and a hearing aid, sat behind a tiny desk, which looked rather lost in the spacious office.

"Hello, young lady. I believe you have some questions

regarding signage?"

"Not so much a question as a complaint."

"I see. Please take a seat and I'll see if I can help you."

"I'd prefer to stand if it's all the same to you."

"As you wish."

"I've just received a letter from your department, and I have to say that I'm absolutely appalled. I can't believe you would inflict these unnecessary costs on the businesspeople of Washbridge. What possible difference can it make to the city council what colour signage a private business displays? For example, my sign has black print on a white background. What's wrong with that, I'd like to know?"

He held up his hand. "If I could just interrupt you for a moment."

"No. Please allow me to finish. I've had all kinds of problems getting my new sign installed, and now you want me to take it down. And you have the cheek to say that if I don't, I'll be fined, and that you'll continue to fine me every month until I comply."

"May I speak now?"

"Sure. Go ahead."

"I have no idea what you're talking about, err—sorry, I didn't catch your name."

"Jill Maxwell."

"I know nothing about this, Mrs Maxwell."

"Really? Well, that's very strange because I received the letter this morning from this very department."

"No, you didn't."

"Are you calling me a liar?"

"I'm simply saying that no such letter has been sent out, and no such regulations have been introduced."

"Are you telling me that signs don't have to be navy blue print on a white background?"

"Not at all. They can be any colour you want them to be. In fact, providing the sign isn't offensive, then it's of no concern to us at all. Yours isn't offensive, is it?"

"Of course it isn't. Are you sure about this, Mr Carter? Could someone else from another department have sent out the letter?"

"I'm positive. I can assure you that any signage-related issue would be dealt with by this department."

What was going on? If the council hadn't sent out the letter, then who had? It was at that precise moment that the penny dropped. I knew exactly where that letter had come from.

"In that case, Mr Carter, I'm very sorry to have wasted your time."

"Not a problem. Is there anything else I can help you with?"

"No, that's everything. Thank you very much for seeing me."

***

I had an appointment with Susan Brown who had worked at the drive-thru at the time of the murder. She lived in a small semi-detached house, which was next door to a funeral director.

A woman in her fifties answered the door.

"Hi, I'm here to see Susan Brown."

"Susan is my daughter. I'm Mary. You must be the private investigator lady."

"That's right. Jill Maxwell."

"Susan's just finished feeding little Charlie, but you can go through. It's the first door on your left."

"Thanks very much."

Susan Brown was on the sofa, trying to wind the tiny little boy. Her hair was dishevelled, and she looked very tired.

"Hi, I'm Susan."

"Thanks for seeing me. I realise this probably isn't a great time. Is he your first?"

"Yeah. Gorgeous, isn't he?"

I glanced at the ugly baby. "Yeah, he's beautiful."

"I believe you've been hired by Arnold's parents."

"That's right. I'm hoping to prove that he's innocent of Alison Reed's murder. I understand from the manager of Wash Burgers that you are one of only a few people who were working at Burger Barn, as it was then, at the time of the murder."

"I'm probably the only one. When the original business closed, everyone was let go. By the time it was sold and reopened, most people had found other jobs. I hadn't managed to get anything else, so I applied for my old job back. I didn't really have any choice."

"Did you know Arnold Kramer well?"

"Probably as well as anyone there knew him. I reckon he thought of me like an older sister who he could confide in. He's a sweet lad who hadn't had a girlfriend before Alison."

"Did you know her?"

"Not really. I did see her with Arnold a few times, and to be honest, I tried to talk him out of the relationship."

"Why would you do that?"

"I shouldn't speak ill of the dead, but I saw the way she

operated. Even when she was with him, she was always flirting with other guys behind his back. I got the impression that she wasn't really into Arnold. He didn't take any notice of me because he was totally smitten, and he wouldn't hear a bad word about her. But then she dumped him."

"How did he take that?"

"Not well at all. He went to a very dark place, and I was really worried about him for a while. I thought he might harm himself. I certainly didn't expect him to hurt Alison."

"Did you think he was capable of doing something like that?"

"Never. But then the evidence presented in court was pretty damning. I do hope they got it wrong and that you're able to prove his innocence. It was a terrible affair, and it wasn't just Arnold who was affected; it destroyed Mickey as well."

"*Mickey*? Sorry, who's Mickey?"

"Mickey Babcock. He owned the restaurant at the time of the murder. He's a really nice guy who was very good with the staff. You could always talk to Mickey. After the murder, the bad publicity had a devastating effect on the business. It never recovered and he was eventually forced to close."

"Who bought it?"

"A guy called Jason Bond who still owns it now. He's the exact opposite to Mickey. Jason is a nasty piece of work. I hate working there now. I wish I didn't have to go back but I need the money."

"This guy, Mickey. Do you happen to know where he is now?"

"I don't have an address for him, but I think he's still living in Washbridge. I've bumped into him a few times; the last time I saw him, he looked as though he'd fallen on hard times. I feel really sorry for him. He didn't deserve what happened."

"Were you on duty the night of the murder?"

"No, it was my night off."

"Did Arnold often work on the window at the drive-thru?"

"There was a rota. On average, I'd guess he was on there a couple of nights each week."

After leaving Susan Brown, I tried Karen Little's number again, but there was still no answer, so I left yet another voicemail.

Chapter 16

I was headed back to the office when my phone rang. When I saw that it was Grandma, my heart sank. If that wart of hers was still playing up, she'd probably want me to apply more of that yucky lotion. I wasn't sure I could face that, but there was no point in ignoring the call because she wouldn't give up.

"Yes, Grandma?"

"Get down to Ever."

"Have you never heard of *please* and *thank you*?"

"Straight away!" She hung up.

That woman was so selfish. It never seemed to occur to her that anyone else might be busy. Everyone was expected to drop whatever it was they were doing and jump to attention.

Still grumbling under my breath, I made my way down to Ever where I found her at her desk. Thankfully, the wart on her nose was back to its normal size, and it was no longer changing colour.

"Your nose is looking much better, Grandma."

"And not before time. It was very embarrassing having to walk around with that beekeeper's hat on my head. Which reminds me—" She reached down into her desk drawer. "Take it back for me, would you?"

"Take it back where?"

"Where do you think? Washbridge Beekeepers' Supplies and Hire, obviously."

"Can't *you* take it back?"

"I would but my feet are giving me gyp. I don't suppose you'd like to massage them, would you?"

"No, definitely not. I'll take the hat back so you can rest

them."

"Make sure you get it back by Wednesday or I'll have to pay for another week's hire."

"Okay. I'm glad your nose is better, and that Rhonda came through for you."

"Hmph! The next time I see that woman, she'll have some explaining to do."

"Why? She came up with the right potion in the end, didn't she?"

"That's typical of you, Jill. You're far too forgiving."

"Nobody could accuse you of that. Incidentally, on my way in just now, I noticed a couple of elderly guys going up to the roof terrace, so I assume you're still selling those dodgy apples."

"There's nothing *dodgy* about them. Look, the main reason I asked you to come down here — "

"*Asked?*"

"Is because I have a bit of an emergency on my hands."

"What kind of emergency?"

"Do you know Julie?"

"Your head Everette? Yes, she's a lovely girl."

"She came in here earlier and handed in her notice. Just like that. Without any consideration as to how it would affect me. Can you believe it? After all the things I've done for her."

"Such as making her wear that awful uniform, and paying her a pittance?"

"She says she's going to leave at the end of next week. So inconsiderate."

"I'm sorry to hear that, Grandma, but I'm not sure what you expect me to do about it."

"I thought you could come and work here for a couple

of weeks until I find a permanent replacement. It's not like you have anything else to do."

"It may have escaped your notice, but I have a business of my own to run, and I'm very busy, as it happens. I don't have time to work in here."

"I'd make you temporary manager and pay you a good wage."

"Sorry, Grandma, I simply don't have the time." And I'd rather chew glass.

"What about that sister of yours? What's her name?"

"It's *Kathy*, as well you know. She wouldn't be interested. Her bridal shops are doing remarkably well, and she's already talking about opening a third one."

"This is all very inconvenient. What am I supposed to do?"

"You could always try putting an ad on one of those job websites."

"Do you have to pay to do that?"

"I would imagine so."

"I suppose I'll have to do that, then." She sighed. "Right, well, you've been no help at all. You can go."

And with that, I was dismissed.

As I left the shop, I spotted Julie behind the counter. She was busy with a customer, so I didn't go over to talk to her, but I did give her a thumbs-up.

***

Back at the office, Mrs V was busy knitting. She'd still not made any mention of what she'd been up to in Coffee Games, so I figured it was personal, and none of my business.

Which made me even more curious.

Winky was sitting on my desk, filing his claws.
"If it isn't pigeon girl!"
"No salmon for you for a month."
"What?" He dropped the nail file. "Come on. Don't you think you're overreacting? It's only a nickname."
"This isn't about pigeon girl."
"Why then? Don't tell me you're broke again."
"It's got nothing to do with the money."
"Why can't I have any salmon, then?"
"Because you sent me on a wild goose chase to Washbridge City Council offices and let me make a complete fool of myself."
"I can't believe you fell for that." He laughed. "But you did, didn't you? Hook, line and sinker."
"I've just wasted an hour of my life down there."
"Come on, Jill. Whatever happened to your sense of humour? I thought for sure you'd see the funny side."
"Well, you were wrong. Let's see if you see the funny side when you're eating budget cat food for a month."
He clearly didn't because he disappeared under the sofa to sulk.

I made a call to the new owner of the drive-thru where the murder had taken place.
"Is that Jason Bond?"
"Jason speaking."
"My name's Jill Maxwell. I'd like to talk to you about the murder of Alison Reed."
"Sorry, darling, who are you exactly?"
"I'm a private investigator. I've been hired by Arnold

Kramer's parents, to try and prove his innocence, and I was hoping I might speak to you?"

"I don't see how I can help, darling. I didn't take over the business until long after the murder took place."

"Still, if you'd just spare me a few minutes."

"No chance, darling. It was the publicity surrounding the murder that resulted in the restaurant being closed down before. I don't intend to do anything that might result in a repeat of that."

"But, Mr Bond, if you could just—"

It was too late; he'd hung up. What a creep. How dare he *darling* me?

Winky was still grumbling to himself and glaring at me from under the sofa. He could keep that up forever as far as I was concerned. He'd pushed me too far this time.

My phone rang.

"Luther, hi. Is everything okay for tonight?"

"Yes and no. I thought I'd better let you know that I've just had a phone call from the restaurant to say they have a problem in the kitchen. Something to do with the cold-room, I believe. They've had to cancel all tonight's bookings."

"Really? How disappointing."

"There's a little Italian place near my offices. I'm pretty sure I'll be able to get a table there, but I wanted to check with you to see if that would be okay."

"That's fine by me. What time?"

"I'll have to see what they have available, but I'll try for eight-ish. I'll send you a text as soon as I've made the booking."

"Okay, that's great. We're both looking forward to

tonight."

***

I'd already interviewed two of the members of the art appreciation society, and I was now on my way to see Myla Donovan.

The woman who answered the door had long, dark hair, and was wearing a full-length floral dress.

"Hi. My name is Jill Maxwell. I phoned earlier."

"Wait there a moment, would you?"

She disappeared back into the house, leaving the door slightly ajar.

Moments later, she reappeared, but this time she was wearing a trouser suit.

"Jill?"

"Err, yeah." Her quick-change routine had left me a little confused.

"Do come in."

It was only when I got inside, that everything became clear. The woman who had originally answered the door was standing in the hall. The two women were obviously identical twins.

"This is my sister, Maureen," Myla said.

"Right. It's nice to meet you both."

"Maureen's just about to leave. Let's go through to the lounge; we can talk in there."

We both took a seat on a large leather sofa, which insisted on squeaking every time I moved.

"I understand that you've already spoken to Hannah and Finley," she said.

"That's right. Did they call you?"

"Actually, we met for drinks last night. We were discussing the missing painting."

"What did you think of the painting?"

"It's a first-class piece of art, but I think it's wasted on Lori. Goodness knows where she found the money to pay for it."

"Can you talk me through what you remember about the day in question?"

"There isn't a lot to tell. We talked in the dining room for a while, and then Lori went to get the drinks. While she was out of the room, the bees somehow got in, and we were forced to leave. Lori called the pest-control man, and the rest of us went home."

"Do you have any thoughts on what might have happened to the painting?"

"Not really. I suppose some lowlife must have sneaked into the apartment while we were outside and stolen it. I heard there had been a spate of burglaries in that area."

After I'd left Myla's, I tried again to contact the remaining member of WFAAS: Gabriella Wilde. I'd called her a few times previously, but she'd not answered my calls. However, as you know, persistence is my middle name, and this time I managed to get through to her.

"Gabriella Wilde?"

"Speaking."

"My name is Jill Maxwell. I'm a private investigator, working for Lori Harty. I wondered if you might be able to spare me a few minutes."

"I'm not sure how I could be of any help, and I am very busy at the moment."

"Like I said, it will only take a few minutes."

"Very well. If we must."

"Thank you. I do appreciate it. If you could give me your address, I'll come—"

"It might be better if we met in a tea room somewhere because I live some distance outside of Washbridge."

"I'm quite happy to travel to your house."

"No." She snapped. "That won't be necessary. Do you know the tea room called Tea Time? It's near the library."

"Yes, I know the one."

"Tomorrow at three?"

"Okay. I'll see you then. How will I know you?"

"I'll have a yellow handbag."

***

I was treading the now familiar path to Candlefield town hall; this time, to upgrade my subscription to include the premium package.

You would have thought that the slim young man with the unusual quiff would have known me by now, but once again, when I walked through the door, he looked at me blankly.

"Hi again," I said. "I recently renewed my spell book subscription, but I now realise that I need the premium package add-on."

"Right, madam. You would have been better off doing that at the same time as you renewed your subscription. It would have been cheaper that way. Only eight pounds."

"How much is it now?"

"Twelve pounds."

"Couldn't I still get the lower price? I only renewed the subscription yesterday. I didn't even know about the premium package."

"I'm afraid that's not possible. The system won't allow it."

"Great."

"Do you still want the premium package?"

"Yes, I don't really have any choice."

"Okay, I just need to complete this form."

He went through the same details again, and then asked me for the cash. And yes, I had remembered to bring it with me.

"Right, that's everything," he said. "I'll just update your subscription on the computer." He tapped a few keys. "Oh?"

"What's wrong?"

"The computer seems to have died." He turned around. "Gillian, is your computer working?"

She checked her screen. "No, it's down."

"What about yours, Roxanne?"

"Mine's down too. It looks like they're all down."

The young man turned back to me. "I'm very sorry, madam, but it seems we have a problem with our computer system at the moment."

"Couldn't I just leave it with you to update the subscription when the computer is back up?"

"Unfortunately, I'm not allowed to do that. For legal reasons, the customer has to be present while the transaction is processed. You're quite welcome to hang around, to see if the system comes back up. Sometimes it only takes a few minutes."

"Okay, I'll wait."

Thirty minutes later, the system was still down.

"I'm going to have to leave it for now." I sighed.

"I'm really sorry about this, madam. These outages don't usually last this long. You're welcome to come back tomorrow."

"Right. It's not like I have anything better to do."

***

As soon as I walked through the door, Ike came rushing down the stairs.

"Sorry, Ike, but I wasn't able to upgrade to the premium package."

"Why not?"

"I tried, believe me. I went to the town hall, filled in the form, handed over the money, but then the computer system crashed."

"Couldn't you have waited for it to come back up?"

"I did, for half-an-hour, but it was still down. It looks like you're going to be here for another night."

"Okay, thanks for trying. Can I borrow your phone to call the missus again? I'm not sure she'll believe me, though. She probably thinks I'm seeing another woman."

It was almost six o'clock and the ruby fairies were scheduled to arrive at any moment.

"This is exciting, isn't it?" Jack said.

"It's certainly the easiest four grand I've ever made, just for putting a few fairies into the airing cupboard for a couple of months. We'll have to be careful we don't forget they're there."

"It'll be fine if we put them on the top shelf, and don't use that shelf for anything else." Jack glanced out of the window where a large white van had pulled up. "I think they're here."

"I don't think that can be them, Jack. Look at the size of the vehicle; it looks like a removal van."

Just then, two men, who I recognised as wizards, got out of the van, went around the back, and opened the doors. The next thing I knew, they were carrying a large box between them up the driveway.

"What's going on?" Jack said.

"I've no idea, but you'd better go upstairs and hide while I answer the door."

"Okay." He dashed upstairs, just as there was a loud knock at the door.

"Are you Jill Maxwell?"

"Yes, that's me."

"We have a delivery for you. I believe you're expecting it."

I glanced at the large box. "I think there may have been a mistake. I'm expecting a delivery of ruby fairies."

"That's what this is."

"Oh? Okay then, you'd better bring it inside."

I could only assume that they must have used a large box with plenty of packaging, in order to keep the tiny fairies safe.

The two men put the box down in the hallway.

"Do you need me to sign anything?" I said.

"Yes, after we've brought in the others."

"*Others?*"

"There are four more outside in the van."

"*Four?*" I had no idea what was going on.

Five minutes later, there were five identical boxes in the hall.

"That's the lot." He handed me a form. "If you could just sign here."

I did as he asked, and they went on their way. Jack must have heard them leave because he came rushing down the stairs, but stopped halfway when he saw the boxes.

"What are those?"

"They said they're the ruby fairies."

"Why are they in such large boxes? They're only tiny, aren't they?"

"Err, yeah, I think so. I assume they must have used lots of packaging to keep them safe."

"Let's open one and take a look." Jack went through to the kitchen and returned with a pair of scissors.

He snipped the parcel tape, and then began to rip open the box. As I'd expected, it was full of straw-like packaging.

Suddenly, Jack took a step back. "What's that?"

"What's what?"

"That. It looks like—err—it's—it's a head." He pulled away more of the packaging. "There's a person in here. A person with wings."

"Oh?"

"They must be three feet tall. This can't be a ruby fairy, can it, Jill?"

"I—err—don't know."

"You said they were tiny."

"I assumed they'd be the same size as starlight fairies, which are teeny little things."

"This definitely isn't teeny. And we have another four of them! What are we supposed to do with them, Jill? There's no way one of these is going to fit in the airing cupboard, never mind five of them."

I took out my phone.

"Who are you calling?"

"Luther. I have to tell him that we need to cancel tonight."

"What will you say when he asks why?"

"I don't know. I can hardly tell him that we've got five oversized fairies in the hallway, can I? I'll think of something."

I went through to the kitchen, rang Luther, and told him that Jack had come down with a tummy bug, that we were sorry, and we'd have to take a rain check. Once I'd finished on that call, I rang the foster agency.

"What did Luther say?" Jack asked when I returned to the hall.

"I told him you had a tummy bug, and that we'd have to get together another day. I've also spoken to the foster people."

"What did they say?"

"She wasn't very pleased when I told her we'd need to return the fairies, but what else could I do? We don't have room for them here."

"When are they going to collect them?"

"They can't do it until the morning."

"What?" Jack looked horrified.

"I wasn't really in a position to argue. After all, we've let them down rather badly."

"What are we going to do with the fairies until then?"

"I asked if it would be alright if we left them in the boxes, but she said they wouldn't be warm enough. We have to find somewhere warmer for them to stay overnight."

"Where?"

"We can put them in our bed, pull the covers over them, and turn the radiator up."

"Where will *we* sleep?"

"I don't know. In the lounge, I suppose."

Jack sighed. "I guess this means that we won't be making four grand."

"It's worse than that. They said they'd have to charge us for the wasted delivery and collection."

"How much?"

"A hundred pounds."

By the time we'd unpacked all five fairies, carried them carefully upstairs to our bedroom, and tucked them in bed, Jack and I were completely shattered.

"This wasn't how I expected to spend this evening," Jack said. "I thought we'd be enjoying a nice meal with Luther and Rebecca. Instead, we're one hundred pounds down, and we're going to have to sleep on the sofa."

"What do you mean *we're* going to sleep on the sofa? It's only big enough for one. You're in the armchair, buddy."

Chapter 17

"My back is killing me," Jack said, as he struggled to get up off the floor.

"Never mind your back. I can hardly move my neck." I sat up on the sofa. "I barely got a wink of sleep."

"At least you had something comfortable to sleep on. This floor is really hard."

"You should have slept in the armchair."

"It's too small. I've got cramp too."

"Stop complaining and go and make breakfast for your darling wife."

He stood up and stretched. "What do you want?"

"I fancy scrambled eggs with lots of brown sauce."

"You don't like brown sauce."

"Who says I don't?"

"I've never seen you eat it before." He yawned. "What time are they coming to pick up the ruby fairies?"

"I'm not sure. The woman I spoke to last night was a bit vague. She said it would be some time between nine and ten this morning."

"I can't stay in for them, Jill. I've got a meeting at nine-fifteen."

"Looks like I'll have to, then. Unless I ask Ike to do it."

"Ike?" Jack looked at me, horrified. "You can't let the living dead answer our door."

"Relax, I was just joking. I'll stay in."

On my way upstairs to take a shower, I looked in on the ruby fairies who were snuggled up and fast asleep. Even though they were much larger than I'd expected, they were still very sweet. If we'd had a spare bedroom, which wasn't full of train sets and zombies, I would have seriously considered keeping them. As it was, there was no chance of that, so I'd just have to kiss goodbye to the four thousand pounds I'd already spent in my head.

After I'd showered and got dressed, I went downstairs, where the scrambled eggs and brown sauce were waiting for me.

It went down a treat.

***

Jack had left for work, and I was waiting for the ruby fairies to be collected. I was just contemplating having another cup of coffee when there was a knock at the door. I looked out of the lounge window, expecting to see the van, but there was no sign of it.

When I answered the door, a young man, wearing a pink and grey striped uniform was standing there; he had a large bag slung over his shoulder.

"Do I have the right house? Are you Jill Maxwell?"

"That's me."

"I'm delivering CandleMag." He took one from his bag.

"What is it?"

"Basically, an ad mag. It's been delivered throughout Candlefield for several years, and now we're extending its reach to include sups who live in Washbridge. As you can imagine, we have to ensure it doesn't get into human hands, so I personally deliver every copy."

"That must be very time consuming."

"It is, but what's the alternative?" He handed the magazine to me. "It'll be delivered every month from now on."

I had nothing better to do, so I sat on the sofa and flicked through the magazine. There were all the usual adverts that you'd expect to find in an ad mag published for humans: Electricians, plumbers, that sort of thing. But, in addition to those, there were lots of specialised ads aimed at sups: Services such as broom repairs, artificial blood banks, potions, etc.

One ad in particular caught my eye: It was for a shop that specialised in the supply of humane traps to catch troublesome sups. Of the many traps listed, one was designed specifically to catch wood nymphs, or as they put it: *those pesky, troublesome wood nymphs*.

Those living in the wood behind Mrs V's house were definitely that. I made a note of the shop's address, so that I could pay them a visit later, to see exactly what they had to offer.

At nine-fifteen, the van that had delivered the ruby fairies the night before pulled up outside the house. When I answered the door, the same two men were standing there.

The older of the two said, "I believe that you've rejected the ruby fairies."

"I never said that I'd *rejected* them. When we agreed to look after them, we had no idea how big they were. We thought they were small, like the starlight fairies."

"Don't you think it might've been a good idea to do some research before you signed up?"

"With hindsight, yes, and if we had a spare bedroom that wasn't otherwise occupied, I'd definitely keep them."

"Hmm. Where are they now?"

"Upstairs in our bed."

"I trust you kept the boxes they were delivered in?"

"I'm afraid we ripped them open."

"I see. In that case, there'll be an additional charge of ten pounds per box."

"Right. That's okay."

He turned to his younger colleague. "Charlie, nip down to the van and get five new boxes, would you?" While Charlie was doing that, the older man turned to me. "Can you show me where the fairies are?"

"Yes, of course. Follow me, please." I took him upstairs to the bedroom. "There they are. Nice and cosy, and fast asleep."

"Okay, you can leave us to it now. We'll pack them away."

"Can't I stay and help?"

"No, madam, it would be better if you went downstairs and left us to do our job."

"Would you like a cup of tea?"

"No, thank you."

Back downstairs, in the lounge, I couldn't have felt any more guilty if I'd tried.

Forty minutes later, and they'd finished packing the fairies into the new boxes. When all five boxes were in the van, the older man came back into the house and knocked on the lounge door.

"Right, madam, if you could just sign this paperwork to say that you've rejected the fairies, we'll be on our way."

"But I told you, I didn't reject them."

"Please, don't make this any more difficult than it needs to be."

"Okay." I signed the form, and they left.

***

I'd made the thirty-mile journey to Longdale Prison more times than I cared to remember, but in all of those visits, I'd never seen a more pathetic figure than the one cut by Arnold Kramer. Pale and drawn, he was sitting opposite me in the interview room, and couldn't or wouldn't make eye contact.

We'd been in there for over five minutes, and he'd yet to say a word.

"Arnold, I know this is difficult for you, but it's important that you answer my questions if I'm going to help."

"What's the point?" He slowly raised his head. "No one believes me. I'm never going to get out of here."

Now that he was facing me, I could see a bruise under his left eye. "What happened there?"

"Nothing." He shrugged. "Nothing that doesn't happen all the time in here. No one likes me."

"Which is why it's important that you answer my questions. That will give me the best chance of proving your innocence and getting you out of here."

"No one cares," he snapped.

"Your parents do. You owe it to them not to give up."

"I can't bear to think what they must be going through." He sobbed.

"They're holding up, but they need you to talk to me. Will you do that?"

"What can you do? It's too late now."

"No, it isn't. Not if I can find out who really murdered

Alison."

"Everyone thinks I did it. The police thought it was me from day one. I told them I would never do anything like that, but they wouldn't listen."

"Will you tell me about your relationship with Alison?"

"What do you want to know?"

"Why don't you start by telling me how you two met?"

"She came into the restaurant one day while I was working there. I was behind the counter, and she started flirting with me. I was flattered. No one had ever done that before. When I took the food to her table, she flirted with me again and asked if I wanted her phone number. I thought she was kidding, but I said yes anyway. She wrote it on my arm and said that I should give her a call. It took me a couple of days to summon up the courage, and I was sure it would turn out to be a fake number, but she answered, and we arranged to go out on a date."

"How did things develop from there?"

"Alison was my first real girlfriend, so I didn't have anything to compare it to. I thought it was going okay, but I know some people didn't."

"Who?"

"My housemate said she was just using me. And then there was a woman who I used to work with at the restaurant. She took me under her wing when I first started work there."

"Do you mean Susan Brown?"

"Yeah. How did you know?"

"I've spoken to her."

"Then you'll know that she thought Alison was taking me for a mug. She told me Alison was always flirting with other guys behind my back. She was probably right, but I didn't really care as long as Alison was still with me."

"How long were you two together?"

"Not long. Just over two weeks."

"And how did it end?"

"I'd arranged to go over to her flat. When I got there, she wouldn't let me in. She said it was over and that she was dumping me."

"Did she actually use those words?"

"Yeah."

"Nice. Did she say why?"

"No, but I'm pretty sure she was seeing somebody else. In fact, I think there was someone else in the flat when I called around, which is probably why she wouldn't let me inside."

"How did you feel when she dumped you?"

"How do you think I felt? I was devastated. I loved her. People say I'm stupid when I say that, but it's true, I did. I asked her to give me another chance, but she just laughed and slammed the door in my face."

"Were you angry?"

"A little, yeah, but mainly I was upset. I would never have hurt her, though. I'd never hurt anyone."

"What exactly happened when she came to the drive-thru on the night she died?"

"I was working at the service hatch when her face popped up at the window. I was shocked."

"Did she speak?"

"Not really. She just asked for extra ketchup. It was like I was nothing to her."

"What did you say?"

"Nothing. I just handed her the food and she drove away."

"One of the most damning pieces of evidence against you is the poison that was found at your house. How do you think that came to be there?"

"I honestly have no idea. I've never bought poison in my life. I wouldn't even know where to get it from. I tried telling the police that, but they didn't want to know."

"If you didn't buy it, someone must have planted it at your house, to frame you. Do you have any idea who would do something like that? Is there someone who had a grudge against you?"

"I can't think of anyone. I've racked my brain, but I haven't been able to come up with a single person who would do something like that."

***

Jimmy and Kimmy had warned me that today was graduation day, and that there would be more clowns around than usual.

As I walked towards the office building, I could see a crowd of them outside the door. I assumed they were chatting before they went inside, but when I got closer, I realised they couldn't actually get through the door. This was the overflow.

"Excuse me," I said. "Can I come through?"

A clown with a green nose, which struck me as rather unconventional, stepped in front of me. "There's a queue here. You'll have to wait your turn. And where's your costume? Breezy and Sneezy made it quite clear we all had to wear them."

"I'm not here for the graduation. My office is at the top of the stairs on the right."

"Sorry, my mistake." He turned to the others. "Everyone, let this lady come through, she works in one of the other offices upstairs."

I managed to squeeze my way through the door, but things were no better inside. The stairs were crowded, two abreast, with clowns. Progress was very slow, as I pushed my way from one step to the next.

I'd almost reached the landing when, on the next to the top step, an argument broke out between two clowns who seemed to be having a disagreement over which was the best supplier of comedy bow ties. The one on the left insisted that Splash-O-Matic was by far the best, but his colleague argued that Soak-You was far superior.

The clown on the right laughed out loud. "How can you claim that Splash-O-Matic is the best? Soak-You is miles better." And to prove his point, he squirted a stream of water, which hit the other clown smack in the face.

Infuriated, the clown on the left retaliated. Unfortunately for me, he did so just as I'd moved onto the same step. At that precise moment, the clown closest to me ducked, and I took the full force of the water in my face. I was saturated.

The clown who had soaked me looked horrified, or at least I think he did. It wasn't easy to tell under all that make-up. "I'm so sorry, lady. I didn't see you standing there."

I was too angry to respond, so I hurried into the office.

"Is it raining, Jill?" Mrs V said. "You're wet through."

"No, it's not raining. I've just been assaulted by a clown."

"There are rather a lot of them out there, aren't there?"

"Too many, in my opinion. But then, even *one* clown is

too many."

I went through to my office where Winky was sitting on the sofa.

"Laugh if you dare," I snapped. "If I hear so much as one titter from you, the salmon ban will be extended to six months."

Chapter 18

Water was still dripping from my hair onto the desk when Mrs V came through to my office.

"Here you are, Jill." She handed me a towel. "This should help."

"Thanks. Where did you get that from?"

"I fought my way through all the clowns to Clown's offices. With all the mess they must make down there, I figured they were bound to have some. I told Jimmy and Kimmy, or should I say Breezy and Sneezy, what had happened to you, and they were quite upset. They said they hoped you wouldn't hold it against them."

"Of course not. It wasn't their fault." I began to rub my hair. "I'm glad graduation day is only once a year, though. Is it still as crowded out there?"

"Yes. If anything, it's even busier. I've never seen so many clowns in my life. The clown school must be doing really well. While I'm here, Jill, do you think I could just have a quick word on another matter?"

"Of course. Grab a seat. Is everything okay?"

"Yes, it's just that there's something I've been wanting to talk to you about for a few days now, and I wasn't sure how to approach it."

"Why don't you just come right out and say it. That's usually the best way."

"This isn't something that has ever happened to me before, so when the man phoned, I was a bit confused at first, particularly when he said he was a headhunter. I thought at first that he was some kind of crazy axeman, until he explained that's what they call someone who works at a recruitment agency. He contacted me because they have a vacancy that he thought was ideal for me. It's a secretarial position at a yarn company in West Chipping."

Out of the corner of my eye, I saw that Winky had jumped onto the sofa and was dancing around in obvious glee. I ignored him.

"Was that the man I saw you with in Coffee Games?"

"Yes. I hope you don't think I've been underhanded in going behind your back."

"Of course not. Have you said you'll take the job?"

"No, I've just told the gentleman that I'm not interested. I'm perfectly happy working here. I'm too old and set in my ways for change. If the opportunity had arisen ten years ago, I'd have jumped at the chance, but now I'm happy to see my days out here."

"Are you absolutely sure? Please don't feel you have to stay for me. I'd miss you terribly, obviously, but I—"

"I'm not staying for you, Jill. I'm staying because this is where I want to be."

"What about the money? They must have offered you a decent salary."

"Money isn't everything, dear. You'll realise that when you're older. Armi has a very good pension, which is more than enough for us to live on."

Winky was now slumped, despondent, on the sofa.

"I realise this is selfish of me, Mrs V, but I'm really pleased that you turned the other job down."

"Me too."

As soon as she'd left the office, Winky jumped onto my desk. "Why didn't you tell her to pack her bags and go?"

"Because Mrs V is a valuable employee of this

business."

"You could have brought Jules back."

"I like Jules, but Mrs V has been with me for a long time, and although *you* may not understand the concept of loyalty, I happen to value it very highly."

"What about my loyalty to you? Does that count for nothing?"

"You wouldn't know the meaning of the word. If someone offered you a better deal — more salmon for example — you'd be off like a shot."

"That's true."

A few minutes later, Mrs V came back into my office.

"You haven't changed your mind about taking the job, have you, Mrs V?"

"No, dear. Of course not. There's a gentleman out there who would like to speak to you. He said it's quite urgent. His name is Max Kirk and I think he said it was something to do with a waxwork."

Oh bum! I'd hoped never to hear from that particular man again.

"You'd better send him in, please."

Judging by his expression, Mr Kirk was none too happy.

"Hello again, Mr Kirk. To what do I owe this unexpected pleasure?"

"Where is it?" he snapped.

"Sorry? Where's what?"

"You know very well what. Your waxwork! What have you done with it?"

"I have no idea what you're talking about. I assumed it was still on display in the new arrivals section of the museum."

"It isn't, as you very well know. It's gone missing."

"Surely, you haven't misplaced it already. That's very careless of you."

"It's been stolen."

"Are you sure? Who would do such—?"

"Please don't play the innocent with me, Mrs Maxwell. I was told that you'd paid a visit to the museum while I was on holiday."

"That's right, I did. I wanted to tell you to take that awful waxwork down. It looks nothing like me."

"You're no doubt already aware that I don't believe that just any Tom, Dick or Jill should be granted a waxwork in the museum. I think they should be reserved for those who have made a real contribution to the arts. But, the powers-that-be ordained that you should have one, and having gone to the time and trouble of making it, I expect it to be on display."

"I'm very sorry, Mr Kirk, I really do wish I could help, but like I said, the last time I saw it, it was on display in the new arrivals section."

"I don't believe you, Mrs Maxwell."

"Are you calling me a liar?"

"Yes, I am. And as soon as I have proof that you stole it, I'll be in touch with the authorities, and I'll insist that the full weight of the law be brought to bear."

And with that, he stormed out of the room.

"He didn't seem very happy," Winky said.

"Apparently not."

"I wonder what would happen if someone was to send him a photograph of a miniature version of that waxwork."

"What are you suggesting, Winky?"

"Just that if he were to receive such a photograph, might that be the evidence he needs to go to the authorities?"

"That sounds suspiciously like blackmail."

"It does, doesn't it?" He grinned.

"What do you want?"

"I won't send that nice gentleman the photograph if you lift the salmon ban."

"You have absolutely no scruples, do you?"

"Scruples? No. Salmon, though, I have plenty of that."

***

I'd ripped the advert for the humane trap shop out of CandleMag. For too long now, I'd been led a merry dance by those wood nymphs, and my attempts to trap them had so far come to nought. Weirdly, although the advert showed an address, it didn't actually give the name of the shop. I assumed that must have been an error in the printing process.

I magicked myself to Candlefield and made my way to the address in question. I'd expected to find a shop with a window full of traps and associated paraphernalia, but what I actually found was a cobbler's shop. Perhaps the advert had not only missed out the name of the shop, but also showed the wrong address. If that was the case, there was a good chance that the owner of the cobbler's shop might have been visited by other people who were equally confused by the ad. Maybe he would know the correct address for the humane trap shop; it couldn't hurt to ask.

The cobbler's shop, which was very small and dimly lit, had the familiar smell of leather and glue. Standing behind the counter was an elderly elf who, at first, I thought had a cigarette in his mouth, but then I realised it was a stick of white chalk.

"Hello, young lady." He took the chalk out of his mouth. "How can I help you today? Are your shoes in need of repair?"

"Actually, I'm just after some information. I ripped this advert out of CandleMag." I handed it to him. "As you can see, it's for a shop that sells humane traps, and the address given is this one. Now that I'm here, I can see that's incorrect, but I wondered if you might know where this particular shop is located."

"You're actually in the right place."

"Oh? But isn't this a cobbler's?"

"It is indeed, but that's not all we do." He came out from behind the counter. "Would you care to follow me?" He walked over to the back wall, which was full of shelves containing all manner of shoe accessories: polish, brushes, laces, and shoehorns, to name just a few. He took hold of one of the brushes and pulled it like a lever. Immediately, a section of the wall slid slowly down into the ground, revealing a passageway.

"This way." He stepped inside and, after a moment's hesitation, I followed him. The walls of the narrow passageway were cold to the touch. Gaslights, high on the wall, illuminated the way as we descended the steep slope. Eventually, we came to a large wooden door. The elf took a key from his pocket, unlocked it, and stepped inside, beckoning me to follow.

The small room was full, floor to ceiling with all manner of contraptions—clearly traps of one type or another.

"Tell me, young lady. What kind of trap is it you're

looking for?"

"I've been having a problem with wood nymphs."

"I'm not surprised." He nodded. "They can be very troublesome. What have you tried so far?"

"I purchased a trap in the human world, baited it with pink marshmallows, which I was assured would attract them, but it didn't seem to work."

"Pink marshmallows will attract them, but that's no good if you don't have the right kind of trap, and that's the WN63. Would you like to see it?"

"Yes, please."

He walked over to the far side of the room and came back with what appeared, to my untrained eye, to be a simple wooden cage, not too dissimilar to the one I'd used before, except that one had been metal.

"There you are. The WN63. Isn't she a beauty?"

"It's very — err — handsome, but it does look rather like the one I tried before."

"Looks can be deceptive. The problem with conventional traps is that they don't take into account the wood nymphs' special abilities. Not many people appreciate that they're able to extend their arms, so they can reach the bait without ever having to step inside the trap."

"I see, but how does this trap address that problem?"

"Allow me to illustrate." He took out a packet of lemon sherbets from his pocket and placed one in the centre of the trap. "For the purposes of this demonstration, I'm going to have to ask you to imagine that's a marshmallow."

"Okay."

"Why don't you reach inside and pick up the sweet."

I hesitated. "It's not going to hurt me, is it?"

"No, you're perfectly safe, I promise. Just reach inside and grab the sweet."

"Okay." I put my arm through the opening, and tried to take it, but no matter how far I reached, the lemon sherbet always seemed to get further and further away. "How is that happening?" I pulled my arm back out.

"That's the WN63's special properties. No matter how far you extend your arm, you'll never be able to reach the bait. The only way the wood nymph can get to it is to climb inside the trap, and when he does, bingo!"

"That's quite ingenious."

"The result of years of research, no less."

"There are three of the little blighters. Will one trap catch all of them?"

"It might, but to be safe, you'd be better using three separate traps."

"How much do they cost?"

"We hire them out; the cost is ten pounds PTPD."

"PTPD?"

"Per trap, per day."

"Right. In that case, I'll take three of them, please."

***

When I arrived at Tea Time, Gabriella Wilde was already seated at a table. I recognised her because, as promised, she had a yellow handbag. I asked if she'd like another drink, but she said she preferred to get straight down to business.

"I can't stay long," she said. "I have a hairdresser's appointment in twenty minutes."

"Okay, I'll make this as quick as possible. As you know, I've already spoken to the other members of the art society. According to them, you all chatted in the dining room for a while, then Lori went through to the kitchen to make drinks. It was at that point that the bees appeared, and you evacuated the apartment. Is that your recollection of the day?"

"More or less, yes."

"Do you attend all the society's meetings?"

"Yes, although I've never particularly enjoyed those held at Lori's."

"Why's that?"

"I find the way she displays her art to be rather tasteless. Have you seen her apartment?"

"Yes, I've visited it."

"Then you'll know what I mean."

"Do I sense a certain amount of animosity towards her?"

"Not towards her personally. I just don't think she fits into the society. She doesn't have the eye for art that the rest of us have."

"What did you think of the painting that was stolen?"

"An excellent piece, but it was totally wasted on Lori."

"Did you see how the bees got into the room?"

"I assume they came through the patio door. Where else would they have come from?"

"And on your way out of the apartment, did you happen to notice if the painting in question was still on the wall?"

"I really couldn't say. I suppose so, but everyone was in such a panic to get away from the bees that I didn't really notice."

"Did you see anyone hanging around the building, either when you arrived or after you'd evacuated?"

"No, the only people I saw were the other members of the society. I have to say, I don't understand what all the fuss is about. It's quite obvious that it was a burglary, and as far as I'm aware, Lori is insured, so she'll be fully reimbursed for the painting. I can't imagine why she felt the need to involve you."

Chapter 19

The next morning, Jack brought me a cup of tea in bed.

"What are you after?" I yawned.

"Why so cynical? I'm not after anything. When I woke up, you looked so peaceful that I didn't like to disturb you, so I thought I'd treat you to a nice cup of tea in bed."

"Thank you." I eyed him suspiciously.

"I slept like a log last night," he said.

"Me too." I took a sip of tea. "I still feel bad about the ruby fairies, but it was nice to sleep in a bed again."

"Even better, we have the house to ourselves at long last."

"Yes, thank goodness. I was so relieved when I managed to get the premium package upgrade yesterday. I was convinced that something else would go wrong."

"Not as pleased as Ike. He couldn't wait to get home to his wife."

"He said he's going to give us some cash to refund the cost of the premium upgrade. I told him it wasn't necessary, but he insisted. And, like he said, we have provided him with bed and board for the last few days."

"That's true. And now that we've lost the ruby fairy cash, we're going to need every penny we can get our hands on. By the way, what are those three small wooden cages in the spare bedroom?"

"I brought those home yesterday. They're humane traps to catch those nymphs that live in the woods behind Mrs V's house."

"Didn't you try to catch those guys once before?"

"Yeah, but the trap I used then wasn't fit for purpose. These were designed specifically to catch wood nymphs."

"Why do you need three of them?"

"Because, according to the guy in the shop, I'd never catch all three of them with a single trap, but if I bait each one with marshmallows, they'll each make for a separate trap."

"And Bob's your uncle."

"Why do people say that?"

"Say what?"

"Bob's your uncle. I don't have an Uncle Bob, and I suspect not many people do."

"I don't know, Jill." Jack sighed. "It's just a saying."

"A stupid one if you ask me."

"No one did. Don't you need marshmallows for the traps?"

"Yes, I'll call at the corner shop for some before I go to work."

"Didn't you say that wood nymphs only eat the pink ones?"

"Yeah."

"In that case, can I have the white ones?"

"Sure, if you give me half the money."

"I brought you tea in bed. Doesn't that count as payment in lieu?"

"No chance, buddy. Cash only."

"Do you have anything else interesting on today? Apart from trapping the wood nymphs, that is?"

"I'm not sure I'd call it interesting, but I am playing chauffeur to Winky tonight."

"Oh yeah." He laughed. "I'd forgotten about that."

"I'm not even sure why I'm taking him. He certainly doesn't deserve it. Not after that prank with the city council letter. I don't know what time I'll be home tonight."

"No problem. I'll probably get myself some fish and chips."

***

After Jack had left for work, I took a walk to the corner shop. I was just about to cross the road when something flashed by me. It took me a moment to realise that it was Janice on her pogo stick. She was going at quite a lick, stopping just long enough to glance both ways before crossing the road.

When I got inside the shop, she was pogoing up and down the fruit and veg aisle. I walked over to where the basket-machine was usually located, but there was no sign of it. Instead, the baskets were simply piled up on the floor.

After grabbing the other bits and pieces I needed, I made for the confectionary aisle, but there was no sign of any marshmallows.

Behind the counter, Little Jack still looked like he was in a wind-tunnel.

"Jack, what happened to your machine with the baskets?"

"I had to give up on it. One minute, it wouldn't give people their money back, and the next it was spraying cash onto the floor like a fruit machine. It was more trouble than it was worth."

"I was looking for marshmallows, but I can't see any on the shelves. Do you have any in the back?"

"I'm sorry, Jill, but I can't get hold of them for love nor money. There's a national shortage."

"Are you being serious?"

"Absolutely. It's been in all of the trade papers."

"But I really need some. It's urgent."

"We have plenty of other sweets you could try. How about some bonbons?"

"Bonbons are no good. I need them for—err—never mind."

Just then, Janice came pogoing up to the counter and stopped next to me.

"Hi there," I said.

"Hello. Isn't it a beautiful day?"

"Actually, I thought it was rather cold."

"I suppose it is, but I don't really feel it when I'm on the pogo stick. It gets the blood rushing through the veins."

"Do you go everywhere on that?"

"Most places, yes. If I'm going into town, I'll sometimes take the bus, but whenever I can, I prefer the pogo stick. It's much healthier and it's cheaper too. Have you tried it?"

"Not since I was a kid."

"Would you like a go now?"

"Err, no thanks. Maybe another time."

***

Mrs V looked happier than she had for several days.

"Good morning, Mrs V. It's nice to see you looking so bright."

"Morning, Jill. I'm just pleased to have put that awful headhunting business behind me. And, I have the house to myself tonight."

"How come?"

"Armi is going to a cuckoo clock conference in Birmingham and he's staying overnight. He asked me to go with him, but to be honest, I'm looking forward to some me-time. Don't get me wrong, I love him to bits, but sometimes you just need time to yourself, don't you?"

"I know what you mean. Men can be such hard work."

Winky barely noticed me walk into the office because he was much too busy trying on one outfit after another.

"I can't decide which one to wear." He was currently sporting a black pinstripe suit. "What do you think of this one?"

"I think you're wasting your time trying those on."

"What are you talking about? I have a great chance of winning tonight."

"That's not what I meant. I'm not sure I'm going to be able to take you."

"Why not? You promised you would, and it's too late to make alternative arrangements now. Is it because of that city council letter?"

"No, it's got nothing to do with that."

"It is, isn't it? I thought you had more of a sense of humour, Jill. It was only a joke."

"I just told you. It has nothing to do with the letter. I have to try to locate some pink marshmallows."

"And you call yourself a private investigator? Duh, let me think. Where might you find marshmallows? How about a sweet shop?"

"I'm not stupid. I know where to buy them, but there's a national shortage, apparently. I'll probably have to spend all day trying to track some down, so I won't have time to chauffeur you around."

"How about if I find them for you?"

"Do you think you can?"

"Of course I can."

"They have to be pink ones."

"No problem. If I find them, do you promise you'll take me to the competition tonight?"

"Yeah, I promise."

"Okay, I'm on it." He took off the suit and then disappeared through the window.

Although I say it myself, blackmailing Winky had been a flash of genius on my part. If anybody could find the marshmallows, it would be him.

A few minutes later, Mrs V popped into my office.

"Sorry, Jill, I meant to give you these earlier." She handed me a box of chocolates.

"Where are these from?"

"Jimmy and Kimmy brought them over. They said it was by way of a thank you for putting up with the graduation day, and also as an apology because you got soaked to the skin."

"That was very nice of them." I opened the box. "Would you like one, Mrs V?"

"I am rather partial to Turkish delight."

"Help yourself. Take both of them."

I popped a chocolate caramel into my mouth, and then put the box in the bottom drawer of my desk, so Winky couldn't get his paws on them.

***

I'd managed to track down Mickey Babcock who had

been the owner of the drive-thru restaurant at the time that Alison Reed was murdered. The resultant publicity had had such an adverse effect on the business, that shortly afterwards, he'd been forced to close down.

Susan Brown had mentioned that the last time she'd seen him, he looked as though he'd fallen on hard times. Judging by the block of flats in which he now lived, she was probably right. The building, which was just outside Washbridge city centre, was run-down and in serious need of repair.

One of the lifts was out of order but, fortunately, the other one was still operational. At least, I thought it was *fortuitous* until I stepped inside; the smell was enough to knock you out. By the time I reached the seventh floor, I was pleased to get out of there and take a breath of fresh air.

I knew that Babcock was in his late thirties, but the man who answered the door looked at least ten years older. He clearly hadn't shaved for several days, and his hair hadn't seen a comb in even longer. I wouldn't have been surprised to learn he'd slept in the clothes he was wearing.

"Mr Babcock?"

"Call me Mickey. Come inside. I apologise for the mess. I haven't been able to tidy up for a few days."

If the hallway was anything to go by, he probably hadn't tidied up for the best part of a month. He led the way into the kitchen, which looked like it was stuck in the seventies.

"Would you like a cup of tea or coffee, Jill?"

I glanced over at the dirty mugs on the side of the sink. "No thanks. I've just had one. I'd prefer to get straight down to business, if that's okay with you?"

"Sure."

"Susan Brown told me that the murder had serious repercussions for your business."

"It feels wrong to complain about my business when a young woman lost her life, but yes, it basically destroyed it. Margins were always very tight, but I was just about scraping through. The TV and newspaper coverage of the murder had a terrible impact on the business."

"And you had to sell?"

"I wish. The bank foreclosed on me. I didn't get a penny. I'm still paying off the other debts, which is why I live in this dump."

"Couldn't you have declared bankruptcy?"

"I could, but I couldn't bring myself to stiff all my suppliers. I'm determined to pay them off no matter how long it takes. I'm working two jobs at the moment, and most of the money I earn goes towards paying off my debts. It's going to take years."

"That's very admirable. Not everyone would do that. Can I ask what you thought of Arnold Kramer?"

"He was a good lad. A hard worker who was very conscientious. Not all of them were; most of them just did the bare minimum."

"What kind of person was he?"

"Very shy. Very quiet. Not very outgoing at all."

"Would you have thought him capable of murder?"

"No, not in a month of Sundays. He was a fragile lad who wouldn't say boo to a goose."

"I assume the police interviewed you after the incident?"

"Yes, but there wasn't much I could tell them because I

wasn't there on the day it happened. It was my day off."

"Were traces of the poison ever found in the restaurant?"

"No, none. That was the most frustrating part for me. I made a point of telling the newspapers and the TV that no poison had been found. I thought if they reported that, it might put the customers' minds at ease, but none of the articles even mentioned it."

"I understand that someone did buy the restaurant eventually?"

"Yes. Jason Bond. That lowlife must have picked it up for a pittance."

"You know the man, then?"

"Oh yes, I know him. He and I were rivals before everything went pear-shaped. He has another restaurant a few miles down the road, and he was my main competition at the time. He's a real nasty piece of work."

"In what way?"

"He tried a few dirty tricks on me."

"Such as?"

"He had his people standing outside our restaurant, handing out flyers for his place. That sort of thing is simply not done. Then there was the time when we had a visit from the health inspector. Apparently, there had been an anonymous report that someone had seen a rat in our dining area. I'm convinced that Jason was behind that too."

"He sounds like a nice guy. Susan Brown isn't very impressed with him either."

"I'm not surprised. I've heard he treats his staff like dirt."

I couldn't help but feel sorry for Babcock. Through no fault of his own, he'd lost everything. I felt a certain amount of admiration too. Not many people would have been prepared to endure the hardship he was suffering in order to repay his debts. Kudos to the man.

Chapter 20

I hadn't made much progress in locating Lori Harty's missing painting. Although I'd spoken to all the members of WFAAS, it occurred to me that I still didn't know anything about the painting itself.

A quick search online turned up an article in The Bugle that related to Lori's purchase of the painting. Although the sum involved wasn't particularly high by national or international standards, it had been significant enough for my favourite newspaper to deem it worthy of coverage. My main takeaway from the article was that Lori had purchased the painting from a Mr Ethan Porter who lived in Macclesfield. I had a lot on my plate, and I couldn't afford the time it would have taken to drive there and back, so I magicked myself to his house.

The man who answered the door had grey, curly hair, and was sporting a large yellow and black bow tie.

"Mr Porter?"

"None other."

"I'm sorry to turn up unannounced on your doorstep like this."

"There's no need to apologise. It's not every day that a beautiful young woman turns up at my door." He laughed. "Many years ago, maybe, but not these days. What can I do for you?"

"My name is Jill Maxwell. I'm a private investigator based in Washbridge. I'm trying to find out what happened to a painting that belonged to my client, Lori Harty."

"The Old Barn."

"Sorry?"

"That's the name of the painting I sold to Lori. I heard that it had been stolen. Do come in. Would you care for a tipple?"

"Not for me, thanks. It's a bit early and besides I'm driving."

"You don't mind if I do, do you?"

"Not at all."

He poured himself a small whisky and downed it in one. "That's better. Now, what can I tell you about the painting?"

"Could I start by asking why you decided to sell it?"

"It's a nice piece, but I rarely hold onto any painting for more than a few years. The enjoyment for me is in finding new pieces that interest me. I needed to raise funds to buy that beauty over there." He pointed to an abstract monstrosity on the wall above the fireplace. "What do you think of it?"

"It's—err—very nice. Some of the people I've spoken to seem to think that Lori paid over the odds for the painting you sold her."

"You may say that, but I couldn't possibly comment." He grinned. "To be honest, I'd resigned myself to accepting a lower price from the others when she contacted me."

"*Others?*"

"Didn't you know? The first approach was a combined one by all of the members of the Washbridge art society."

"Including Lori?"

"Yes."

"I wasn't aware of that."

"Apparently, they occasionally pitch in together to purchase a painting, which they then take turns to keep."

"Like some sort of timeshare?"

"I suppose so. Curious idea, but it takes all sorts, I guess. The five of them came to look at The Old Barn. They made me an offer, but it was less than the asking price, so I told them I'd need twenty-four hours to think about it. By the next morning, I'd more or less decided I would accept their offer, but then I had a call from Lori. She said she'd pay the full asking price, provided that I'd agree to the sale there and then. Needless to say, I bit her hand off."

"I see. Did you get the impression that the others knew what she was doing?"

"I didn't ask. I just took her money."

***

For some reason, the episode with the bees was still bugging me.

Bees. Bugging me. Get it? Sheesh! All this effort is wasted on you lot.

Whether by accident or design, it was clear that the bees had provided a diversion for the thief to steal the painting, but how had they got inside the apartment? Bees don't just appear from nowhere, and yet Lori Harty had told me that the pest control man had found no sign of a nest.

I wanted to speak to him myself, to see if he had any other bright ideas about where the bees might have come from. Lori had given me his business card, so I gave the company a ring.

"Pest Out, Sandy speaking. How may I help you today?"

"Hi, my name is Jill Maxwell. I was given the name of

one of your operatives, a man by the name of Craig Fleabit."

"Right?"

"Would it be possible for me to speak to him, please?"

"I'm afraid he's out on calls at the moment. He's likely to be tied up for most of the day, but I can put you through to another of our operatives. I'm sure they'll be able to help."

"If you don't mind, I'd prefer to speak to Craig."

"As you wish, madam. If you give me your number, I'll get him to call you. I should warn you, though, that it may be tomorrow."

"That's fine."

***

Back at the office, I made a phone call to the Kramers.

"Mrs Kramer, it's Jill Maxwell."

"I hope you have some good news for us, Jill."

"I don't have anything to report at the moment, I'm afraid. I was wondering if you get regular phone calls from Arnold?"

"Yes, he telephones every day at three o'clock. Why?"

"Could I possibly sit in on today's call, just for a couple of minutes. There's something I forgot to ask when I visited him."

"Yes, of course, Jill. Why don't you come around this afternoon?"

"Great. I'll see you later."

***

Winky jumped in through the window, and to my delight, he was carrying two bags of marshmallows.

"You did it!"

"Was there ever any doubt?" He shrugged.

"Well done, you." I took the bags from him. "Where did you get them?"

"That's for me to know and you to wonder."

"These are all pink. I've only ever seen them in bags of white and pink mixed."

"I assume this means you'll keep your end of the bargain and take me to the competition tonight?"

"Of course I will. I'm a woman of her word. But right now, I need to nip out to set the wood nymph traps."

As Armi was away, this was my golden opportunity to go after those wood nymphs. With the three traps in the boot of the car, I drove to Mrs V's house, and parked a little way down the road, so as not to draw attention to myself. The traps weren't particularly heavy, but they were awkward to carry, so for ease, I shrank them, and popped them into my pocket.

I edged around the side of the house and checked the treeline to make sure that the wood nymphs weren't around. Once I was happy the coast was clear, I restored the traps to full-size and placed them on the ground near to the trees. After setting each one with bait, a handful of pink marshmallows, I made my exit. I planned to collect them just before Mrs V finished for the day by which time, hopefully, they would contain the three pesky wood nymphs. I still had a few marshmallows left in my bag, just in case I needed to try again another day.

***

Without a shadow of a doubt, the most damning piece of evidence against Arnold Kramer was the poison found at his home. This had only come to light when a cat had died after ingesting it. The man who Arnold had shared the house with, a Mr Roy Sissons, had understandably been distraught at the horrific death of his pet. It had been Sissons who had reported the incident to the police. Shortly after that discovery, Arnold had been charged with Alison's murder.

Roy Sissons was still living in the house he had once shared with Arnold Kramer. Now, though, he lived there with his new wife, Siobhan.

"Hi, I'm Roy. Come on in."

"Thanks."

"Siobhan has gone into town to do a little shopping. I thought it would be best if we talked alone. Let's go through to the living room." He led the way. "Would you like a drink? It's Jill, isn't it?"

"That's right. No, I'm fine, thanks."

"Err, how is Arnold?"

"Not great. He's ill-equipped to handle prison life."

"I feel terrible about what happened, and the part I played in it."

"You won't be surprised to learn that Arnold still maintains his innocence, which is the reason I'm here today."

"If there's anything I can do to help him, I'm more than happy to."

"You could start by telling me exactly what happened

the day you found the poison."

"Sure. I came home from work at the usual time. Normally, Molly, that was my cat's name, would come running up to me before I'd even reached the front door. On that day, though, there was no sign of her. I wasn't particularly worried because she did occasionally go further afield. An hour later, and there was still no sign of her, so I went out into the back garden to call her. That's when I saw her, down near the shed. She was still alive, making a terrible whimpering noise. She was writhing in agony, and there was foam coming from her mouth. I ran inside and called the vet, but by the time he got here, Molly was dead. He told me it was a classic case of poisoning. I couldn't understand it because we didn't keep anything like that in the house."

"I can understand you being upset, but why didn't you wait until you'd had the chance to speak to Arnold before calling the police?"

"I wish I had, but like you said, I was upset and angry. I knew that Alison had been poisoned, and I put two and two together and got five. If I'd stopped to think about it, I would have known Arnold could never do anything like that."

"I assume the police sent someone around?"

"Yeah, straight away. They searched the house and had people out in the garden. That's where they found the poison."

"In the garden?"

"Yes, it had been buried in a bag near to the shed. The bag had a small hole in it and some of the powder was above ground. The police reckoned Molly must have got it on her paws and tried to lick it off."

"What did you think when you heard that Arnold had been charged with Alison's murder?"

"I was horrified. In court, when I was called to the witness box, I tried to make the point that I didn't think Arnold would ever do anything like that, but it didn't do any good. Do you think you'll be able to get him out of prison?"

"I don't know. So far, I've not found anything that is likely to get his conviction overturned."

***

I arrived at the Kramers' house at five to three.

"Come on in, Jill." It was Mrs Kramer who greeted me at the door. "Arnold should be calling in a few minutes." She led the way through to the dining room where Mr Kramer was waiting by the phone. This was clearly a daily routine for the two of them.

"What is it you want to ask Arnold?" Mr Kramer said.

Before I could respond, the phone rang. It was Mr Kramer who answered it, to a recorded message that asked if they were prepared to accept a reverse charge call from an inmate at Longdale Prison.

"Mum? Dad?" It was Arnold's voice. He sounded a little brighter than when I'd visited him.

"Hello, darling," Mrs Kramer said. "How are you?"

"Oh, you know, the same."

"Hi, champ," his dad said. "We have Jill Maxwell here with us."

"Oh? Hey, Jill."

"Hi, Arnold. Can I ask you a quick question and then I'll leave you to talk to your parents?"

"Sure, fire away."

"On the night in question, do you happen to remember exactly what food you served to Alison?"

"How is that relevant?" Mr Kramer said, but his wife shushed him.

"Actually, I do," Arnold said. "She ordered a burger, a cheeseburger and two Cokes."

"That sounds like an order for two people. Was there anyone with her in the car?"

"No, she was by herself. I assumed she must be meeting Kevin."

"Thanks, Arnold. That's all I need. I'll leave you to talk to your Mum and Dad."

Chapter 21

If there was no one else in the car with Alison Reed on that fateful night, why had she ordered two meals? Who was the other one for? Arnold Kramer had assumed that she must be meeting Kevin Hayes, the guy who she'd dumped Arnold for. I needed to check if that was the case or not, so I called Kevin, but I wasn't able to reach him.

Frustrated, it occurred to me that there was one other person who might be able to clear up this matter, and that was the detective who'd been in charge of the case, Walter Staniforth. Middle Tweaking wasn't too far out of my way, so I turned the car around and headed out there.

As I pulled into the village, I noticed a For Sale sign outside the old watermill, and curiosity got the better of me.

"Jill, what a pleasant surprise." Myrtle had a mousetrap in her hand. "Do come in."

"I won't, thanks. I'm actually on my way to see Walter, but I noticed the For Sale sign as I drove past."

"It went up yesterday."

"That was quick. When I spoke to you last week, you said you were only thinking about the possibility of moving."

"It all happened really quickly. The day after I saw you, I came across a little property on the coast that looked ideal. On a whim, I popped over there to take a look at it. The village is beautiful, and the cottage is everything I could have hoped for. There were a few other interested parties, so I had to make a decision there and then, or I would have lost it. For once in my life, I threw caution to the wind, and told them I'd take it."

"You shouldn't have any problems selling this place."

"I hope not, but I thought I'd better get rid of the mice before anyone comes to view it." She grinned.

"How have Hodd and Jobbs taken the news?"

"Not particularly well. After I told them, they didn't speak to me for twenty-four hours, but they seem to have come around now."

"What will they do? Where will they go?"

"I don't know. There's been some talk about them moving to London, but I have a sneaking suspicion they might turn up on my doorstep again."

"How would you feel about that?"

"I wouldn't mind. They've become part of the furniture. While I was over there, I noticed a few small properties to rent; one of those might be suitable for them."

"I'm really pleased for you, Myrtle, but you mustn't leave without saying goodbye."

"Of course not. It'll probably be months yet. You know how long these things can take."

"I hope everything goes smoothly for you. Anyway, I'd better get going."

I hadn't bothered to call Walter Staniforth in advance, so I had my fingers crossed that he would be in.

He was.

"Jill? I didn't expect to see you again so soon."

"I wondered if I could pick your brain about something related to the Kramer case that I didn't think to ask before?"

"Of course. What is it?"

"Do you happen to remember any details about the meal that Arnold Kramer served to Alison Reed that night?"

"I can remember it was laced with poison." He grinned.

"But do you recall exactly what he served to her?"

"Not offhand. A burger? Fries? Why?"

"Alison ordered a burger and a cheeseburger."

"She must have been very hungry."

"And *two* Cokes."

"I'm not sure what you're getting at."

"It was quite clearly a meal for two people, and yet, there was no one else in the car with her. Don't you find that strange?"

"To be perfectly honest, Jill, we were more focussed on the poison that we'd discovered at Kramer's house. The very same poison that killed Alison."

"Can you remember if you tried to find out who the other meal was for?"

"I'm not sure. Probably. Whoever it was intended for was remarkably lucky. If Alison hadn't decided to tuck into her meal on the way home, they might have suffered the same fate."

Much as I would have liked to press Staniforth further, I got the distinct impression that there was nothing more to be gained. It seemed to me that once the poison had been found at Arnold Kramer's house, the detective was convinced of his guilt, and had become blinkered to the possibility of other perpetrators.

It was now more urgent than ever that I speak to Kevin Hayes. I needed to know if that second meal had been intended for him. If that was the case, and he had been expecting to meet Alison that night, why hadn't he mentioned that when I'd spoken to him? On the other hand, if the meal wasn't for him, who had Alison bought it for?

***

Back at the office, Mrs V wasn't at her desk. I assumed she must have nipped to the loo. That was until I went through to my office where I found a note from her on my desk. She'd been feeling a little queasy, so she had gone home.

Oh bum!

"Winky! How long ago did she put this on my desk?"

Still half asleep, he looked at me with a heavy eye. "How long ago did *who* put *what* on your desk?"

"Mrs V. When did she put this note on my desk?"

"I don't know. I've been asleep."

"A fat lot of good you are."

This was bad. This was really bad. What would she think if she got home and found the traps? Worse still, what if the wood nymphs were inside them? There was no time to drive over there, so I resorted to magic.

Fortunately, when I got to Mrs V's house, there was no sign of her.

Phew!

I hurried around the back, and to my delight, I discovered that each of the traps was occupied by a wood nymph.

"Hey, you! Let us out of here!" William Twigmore screamed at me.

"Sorry, no can do."

I was just about to collect the traps when I heard a voice behind me.

"Jill, what are you doing here?"

Oh bum!

"Mrs V? I—err—I found your note and wanted to check that you were okay."

"You really didn't need to do that, dear. It's just a bit of a stomach bug. I'll be fine when I—" Her words drifted away when she spotted the cages.

"Mrs V? Are you okay?"

"What are those things?"

"What are what?"

"Those strange looking creatures in those cages?"

"Oh, those. They're—err—"

I'm pretty nimble on my feet, but even I couldn't come up with a plausible story to explain away the wood nymphs, so I did the only thing I could. I cast the 'forget' spell on Mrs V and then made a quick exit.

***

By the time I made it back to the office, Winky was in a complete flap.

"Where have you been?" He snapped. "And what are those ugly things?"

"I've been to Mrs V's house and these are wood nymphs."

"Who are you calling ugly?" Twigmore pointed a threatening finger at Winky. "When I get out of here, you'll be dead meat."

"Shut up, you!" I said, and then I made a phone call to Daze. "It's Jill. I need a big favour. Could you come over to my office now?"

"No problem. I'll be there in ten minutes."

"We're going to be late for the competition." Winky tapped his watch.

"No, we're not. I can't leave until I've sorted these guys out. Have you decided which suit you're going to wear tonight?"

"Yes." He unzipped the suit carrier. "I thought I'd go for the black pinstripe. What do you think?"

"Good choice. I like it."

"Let us out of here!" Twigmore yelled.

"I won't tell you again. Be quiet!"

Daze arrived with Blaze in tow.

"Who do we have here?" Daze glanced at the wood nymphs.

"This is William Twigmore and his brothers. They've been stealing food from Mrs V, and generally making a nuisance of themselves."

"That's a wicked lie!" Twigmore protested.

"You can tell that to the court." Daze threw her net over the three cages, and the wood nymphs disappeared in a puff of smoke.

"Thanks, Daze," I said.

"My pleasure. I wish we could find those ice nymphs and do the same thing with them."

"No luck yet, then?"

"Not a sniff."

"I'm sorry but I have to be making tracks. I promised to take Winky somewhere."

"No problem. We're just on our way to get a coffee, anyway."

"Come on, Jill." Winky tapped his watch again. "We'll

never make it at this rate."

"Why don't I magic us there? It'll be much quicker."

"No way." He shook his head. "That magic stuff does weird things to me, and I need to be on tip-top form for tonight's competition."

Winky put the suit carrier on the back seat of the car, and then jumped in next to me.

"I don't even know where we're supposed to be going." I started the engine.

"The competition is being held at Catbert Hall."

"I've never heard of it. Where's that?"

"Directly behind The Albert Hall, obviously."

"*Obviously.*"

Fortunately, the traffic on the drive down to London wasn't too bad, and we arrived with an hour to spare.

Winky grabbed his suit carrier from the back seat and said, "I'll see you back here at ten."

"Hold on. I'll come with you."

"You said you didn't want to."

"I didn't realise it was going to be so cold. I'm not wandering the streets of London in this weather."

"Can't you just go and sit in a coffee shop or something?"

"I want to see the competition."

"Women. I'll never understand them. Come on, then. You'll have to change yourself into a cat first, or you won't get in."

I found a quiet alleyway and did just that.

The cat on reception said that all competitors and their

guests should report to the changing rooms, which were through the first door on the left. It was already full of cats, all preening themselves, and trying on their outfits.

"It looks like you have some stiff competition, Winky."

"This crowd?" He scoffed. "I don't think so."

Just then, a big black cat came over to us.

"Well, well, well, if it isn't Winky."

I could tell by Winky's expression that these two had a history, and not a good one.

"Hello, Winston, what do you want?"

"I just thought I'd come over and offer my commiserations."

"For what?"

"Losing out to me today, of course. The best you can hope for is runner up."

"Dream on, buddy. Now, if you don't mind, I'm busy."

"Of course. I'll see you later. You can come and admire my trophy."

"He's a bit much, isn't he?" I said, after the black cat had walked away.

"That's Winston the Wag. He won last year. I wouldn't say it in front of him, but he's definitely my main competition." Winky spotted someone across the room. "There's Trevor the Tails. I'll just go and say hello. Will you be okay here?"

"Sure."

There wasn't much doing in the changing rooms, so I sneaked out, to take a peep at the front of house: It was a magnificent venue, and the audience were just starting to take their seats.

"Excuse me." A Siamese cat tapped me on the shoulder. "You can't be here. You need to get back to the changing rooms."

"Okay. Sorry."

When I got back there, Winston was hovering close to where Winky had left his suit carrier. I watched in disbelief as he unzipped it. Before I could do or say anything, he'd run his claws down the suit. He then re-zipped the carrier and walked away. What a despicable character. Winky would have no chance of winning with his suit torn to shreds. I simply couldn't stand by and let that happen, so I used the 'take it back' spell to repair the suit.

A few minutes later, Winky returned. I didn't mention the 'Winston' incident because I thought it would upset him ahead of the competition. When the competitors were called to the stage door, the expression on Winston's face was a picture, as he tried to work out how Winky's suit could look so sharp.

Little did he know there was an even bigger surprise awaiting him.

Tee-hee.

I made my way to the front of house and grabbed one of the few spare seats. As each competitor was called, they did a slow circuit of the stage to show off their finery, and then they joined the compere for a brief interview.

Winky's friend, Trevor the Tails, looked really sharp in a silver-grey suit. Winky too was on top form. When they called Winston's name, he began his promenade very confidently, but grew more and more uncomfortable. That may or may not have had something to do with the fact that his suit was slowly shrinking. By the time he reached the compere, it was several sizes too small for him, and he looked quite ridiculous. Clearly embarrassed, he turned tail and hurried off the stage.

Half an hour later, the judges had finished their deliberations. I was backstage with Winky who was clearly nervous.

"What happened to Winston?" I said, all innocent-like.

"No idea." He laughed. "I think he must be using the wrong dry cleaner."

"Ladies and gentlemen." The compere took to the mic. "We now have the results of this year's Best Dressed Cat Competition. In third place is Stewart the Smooth."

Everyone applauded as Stewart, dressed in an unusual tartan suit, went on stage to collect his trophy.

"In second place is Winky."

Winky's face fell, but only for a moment. He quickly recovered and hurried onto the stage.

"And now, ladies and gentlemen, it gives me great pleasure to announce that this year's winner of the Best Dressed Cat Competition is –" Pause for dramatic effect. "Trevor the Tails."

Everyone applauded loudly, including Winky who looked genuinely pleased to see that his friend had won.

Chapter 22

Jack had been forced to work late the previous day, so I'd been fast asleep when he came home. We were catching up over breakfast.

"How did Winky take coming in second place?" Jack was trying to get the last few specks of jam out of the jar.

"Remarkably well, surprisingly. I thought he'd be sulking all the way home, but he was quite philosophical about the whole thing. It probably helped that he lost out to a friend of his, Trevor the Tails. It would have been a different story if he'd come second to that Winston character."

"Who's Winston?"

"A big black cat who tried to shred Winky's suit. He got his comeuppance, though. Inexplicably, his suit began to shrink on stage. He was so embarrassed."

"*Inexplicably*? Hmm. What about those wood nymphs you were trying to catch? How did you get on?"

"Great. Those new traps worked like a dream. I caught all three of them. Mind you, I had a close call while I was doing it."

"Why? What happened?"

"I set the traps early in the afternoon, and I'd planned to collect them just before Mrs V finished for the day, but when I got back to the office, she'd already left because she had a bit of an iffy tummy."

"What did you do?"

"I didn't have much choice. I had to magic myself back to her house, so I could collect the traps before she got home. I assumed they'd still be empty, but the wood nymphs were already trapped inside them, and they weren't happy. I'd just collected the traps when I heard Mrs V's voice behind me."

"Whoops!" Jack laughed. "How on earth did you manage to talk your way out of that one?"

"There was no way I could. I had to cast the 'forget' spell on her."

"What about the wood nymphs? What happened to them?"

"I took them back to the office. Winky wasn't very impressed with them, and they looked like they wanted to rip his throat out. I gave Daze a call and she came over and took the horrible creatures back to Candlefield."

"All's well that ends well, then." Jack stood up. "I'd better be making tracks."

"Before you go, you haven't forgotten that we're having dinner tonight with Swotty Dotty and her partner, have you?"

"I do wish you wouldn't call her that, Jill. What happens if you forget yourself, and say it to her face tonight?"

"What do you take me for? Of course I won't."

***

I wasn't sure if Mrs V would make it into work, but she was behind her desk, looking quite bright.

"How are you feeling, Mrs V?"

"Much better, thanks, Jill. I think I must have eaten something that disagreed with me. Now I come to think of it, it was probably those olives. I overdid it somewhat."

"I didn't realise you liked olives."

"I rarely eat them, but I was out with an old friend of

mine, Olive Cartwright. She's a big fan of the olive. They're probably also the reason for the strange dream I had last night."

Is there anything more boring than listening to someone else talk about their dreams?

"It was really weird," she continued, oblivious to my pained expression. "You were in my back garden, and you were carrying these strange cages with ugly creatures inside them."

"That does sound weird. I think you're right. You'd better stay away from the olives in future."

Winky was on the sofa, clearly half asleep.

"Good morning, Winky."

He stretched and yawned. "Morning."

"I have to say that I was very impressed by the way you handled defeat last night."

"I wouldn't exactly call it a *defeat*."

"Well, unless I'm misremembering, you came in second, didn't you?"

"I did, but technically I won."

"What do you mean, *technically you won*? You came second."

"When I talked to Trevor the Tails, he told me that he'd been having a bit of a hard time. His old mother died recently, and he's been out of work for a while. The poor guy was really down on his luck, so I thought he could do with cheering up."

"Are you trying to tell me that you threw the competition?"

"Let's just say that I had a quiet word with the judges."

"If that's true, how come you never mentioned any of

this on the way home last night?"

"I was too tired."

"I'm not sure that I believe you."

"Please yourself. It makes no difference to me. I know the truth and that's all that matters."

I really didn't know what to make of that. Either Winky was much more selfless than I'd given him credit for, and he'd been exceptionally kind to a friend who had fallen on hard times. Or he was a lying little toad.

What was that croaking sound I could hear?

"Before you go back to sleep, Winky, where's my twenty percent cut of your winnings?"

"Oh yeah." He reached under the sofa and brought out an envelope. "It was three thousand for second place."

"That's six hundred you owe me, then."

"I can count, thanks." He reached inside the envelope and passed me — err — what?

"What are these?"

"Feline vouchers."

"I want cash, not stupid vouchers."

"I said I'd give you twenty percent of my winnings. That's what I won."

"They paid you in vouchers?"

"Yeah. Didn't I mention that?"

"No, you didn't. What am I supposed to do with them? They're no good to me."

"I'll buy them off you."

"Oh? Okay, then."

"I'll give you fifty quid for them."

"But, they're worth six hundred."

"Not if you can't spend them, they're not."

***

I'd finally managed to get hold of Kevin Hayes.

"Sorry, Jill, my phone's been on the blink. I had to take it in to get it repaired. How can I help?"

"On the night that Alison was murdered, had you arranged to meet her?"

"No. Why do you ask?"

"It appears that she ordered two meals, and I thought that maybe one of them was intended for you."

"No, it definitely wasn't for me. But like I said when you and I spoke before, I was sure she was seeing someone else behind my back. Maybe the second meal was for him."

"Do you have any idea who that might have been?"

"Sorry. Not a clue."

"Okay. Thanks, Kevin."

I'd no sooner finished on the call to Kevin than my phone rang.

"This is Karen Little. I have a few messages that you've been trying to contact me. I've been abroad and I've only just got back."

"Thanks very much for calling. The reason I wanted to speak to you is that I understand you and Alison Reed were best friends."

"That's right. Sorry, but who are you exactly?"

"I'm a private investigator. I've been hired by Arnold Kramer's parents."

Her attitude changed immediately. "In that case, I'm not sure I should be talking to you."

"I just need you to spare me a few minutes of your

time."

"Why? Arnold murdered Alison and now he's where he should be: In prison."

"But what if someone else killed her?"

"They found poison at his house, didn't they?"

"Please, Karen, just a few minutes of your time, that's all I ask."

"I'm at work at the moment."

"I can come to you. Do you get a break?"

"I have a fifteen-minute break at three. I could see you then, I suppose."

My phone was red hot today. I'd no sooner finished talking to Karen Little than it rang again.

"Jill, this is your grandmother speaking."

Just what I needed.

"Hello, Grandma. How are you?"

"If I was to tell you all my ailments, young lady, we'd be here all day. The reason I called was to make sure that you remembered to return the beekeeper's hat yesterday?"

"*Yesterday?*"

"Yes, like I asked you to."

Oh bum!

"Yes, of course I did. All done and dusted."

***

Karen Little worked on the cosmetics counter in Washbridge Department Store. We'd agreed to meet in the coffee shop, which was located on the second floor. She said that I'd recognise her because she had a black bow in her hair. Why she didn't think to mention that she had green hair was something of a mystery.

"Karen?"

"Jill? I don't have very long; I only get a fifteen-minute break."

"I understand." I slid onto the seat opposite her.

"I'm not very comfortable with this," she said. "Alison was my best friend, so I don't want to do anything that might help her murderer."

"I can understand that, but you want to ensure that the right person is punished for her murder, don't you?"

She shrugged. "What do you want to know?"

"How would you describe Alison?"

"She was fun; the life and soul of the party. I used to wish I could be more like her."

"What about boyfriends? Before Arnold Kramer, I mean?"

"What about them?"

"Did she have many?"

"A few, yeah, but there's nothing wrong with that."

"Of course not. I was just wondering if there was ever anyone *special* in her life. Someone she went out with for more than just a few weeks?"

"No. Alison was the love 'em and leave 'em type. That's what she used to say, anyway."

"You testified that you'd heard Arnold Kramer make threats against Alison after they broke up?"

She hesitated. A little too long for my liking.

"Yeah, I—err—"

"Karen, you have to be honest with me. If Arnold is innocent, it means that Alison's killer is still walking the streets and might do the same thing to someone else."

"I don't want to get into trouble."

"Why would you get into trouble?"

"You're not supposed to lie in court, are you?"

"Are you saying that you didn't see Arnold threaten Alison?"

"No."

"Why did you say you did? Because you thought Arnold might get away with it if you didn't?"

"No. It wasn't that."

"What then?"

She began to cry. "I'm sorry."

"Come on, Karen. You'll feel better if you tell me. I promise."

"I'd only been in this job for a couple of months. It was my dream job. But the thing is, I hadn't been completely honest on my application form. I hadn't mentioned that I had a conviction for shoplifting from a few years earlier. I assumed they'd do a check, find out about the conviction, and reject my application. But they can't have checked because they gave me the job."

"Okay. I don't see what that has to do with your testimony, though."

"He said if I didn't testify, that he'd tell my employer about the shoplifting."

"*He*?"

"The detective."

"What was his name?"

"I don't know. The old guy who was in charge of the case."

"Right."

"I'm not going to get in trouble, am I?"

"No. You've done the right thing. What did you think of

Arnold?"

"I couldn't see what Alison saw in him. He certainly wasn't her usual type."

"When you say he wasn't her *usual type*, what do you mean by that?"

"She normally went for the bad boys—loud and full of themselves. Arnold was a bit of a drip. I was surprised it lasted as long as it did."

"After they'd broken up, I believe she started going out with a guy called Kevin Hayes. Did you know him?"

"I met him a couple of times, but I wouldn't say that I knew him. Alison wasn't very taken with him either. A few days before she was murdered, she'd told me that she was fed up of him and that she was seeing someone else."

"Behind his back?"

"Yeah, I think so."

"Do you know who it was?"

"No, she didn't tell me his name."

"Was that unusual? For her not to share that with you, I mean?"

"A little. She did say he was quite a bit older than her, and that he had a few annoying habits, but he was minted."

"What kind of annoying habits?"

"Apparently, he's always looking at himself in the mirror, and he insists on calling every woman he meets *darling*."

"I see. And when the police interviewed you, did you mention this other guy to them?"

"Yeah, but they didn't seem very interested, to be honest. The only thing they wanted to talk about was Arnold." Karen checked her watch. "I have to go now. I need to sort out my face before I go back behind the counter."

"Okay. Thanks very much for speaking to me. I really appreciate it."

It had taken some time to get hold of Karen Little, but it had been worth the wait. Her evidence was dynamite. If she was now telling the truth, it seemed that she had been pressured into perjuring herself in order to incriminate Arnold Kramer. And crucially, I also now knew who the other man in Alison Reed's life had been.

***

I was on my way to return the beekeeper's hat. I should have taken it back the previous day, but I'd been so busy that I'd forgotten all about it. Surely, if I explained the circumstances, they'd be understanding.

Washbridge Beekeepers' Supplies and Hire was a small shop behind the police station. I'd actually walked past it several times in the past, and seen the pictures of bees on the window, but as I'd never noticed the name on the sign, I'd always assumed they sold health food: Honey, that type of thing.

Inside, the shelves were full to bursting with all manner of equipment and clothes for the beekeeper. At the counter, a jolly man in his mid-fifties greeted me with a smile.

"Hello there, young lady. I'm Jimmy Bee but everyone calls me Sting."

That just had to be a wind-up.

"Hi."

"Are you an apiarist?"

"Sorry?" Who was he calling an ape?

"A beekeeper? I don't think I've seen you in here before."

"Me? No."

"Don't worry. We'll soon make one out of you. I have just the thing for you: Sting's Starter Kit which includes a hive, frames, smoker, suit, gloves and shoes. And, you'll be pleased to hear, it's very competitively priced."

"Actually, I'm just here to return this." I took the beekeepers' hat out of my bag and handed it to him.

"I see." He made a note of the number on the inside of the hat, and then checked his computer. "This should have been returned yesterday."

"I'm sorry about that. My grandmother was the one who hired it; she asked me to return it yesterday, but I forgot. I suppose that kind of thing happens all the time, doesn't it?"

"Actually, no. Most people return the goods in a timely manner."

Burn.

"Anyway, like I said, I'm sorry."

"That's alright, but it's going to cost you extra."

"Fair enough. What's the PHPD cost?"

"The what?"

"The per hat per day cost?"

"Unfortunately, we don't hire out anything for less than a week, so you'll have to pay for an additional week I'm afraid."

"That's a bit steep, isn't it?"

"You are of course welcome to keep it for another six days and it won't cost you anymore."

"There isn't much point. It's not like I'm going to use it." I handed over the money, and I was just about to leave the shop when, out of the corner of my eye, I spotted a familiar face. The woman was looking around the clothing section of the shop. Fortunately, she hadn't seen me.

I'd no sooner left the beekeeper shop, than my phone rang.
"Is that Jill Maxwell?"
"Speaking."
"This is Craig Fleabit from Pest Out. You left a message for me to call you."
"That's right. Thanks for getting back to me. Actually, I'm just after some information. Do you remember being called out to an apartment block recently where there was an infestation of bees in the dining room?"
"I do, as it happens. Why?"
"Do you know where the bees came from?"
"I've no idea. There definitely wasn't a nest anywhere around the apartment block."
"Are you certain about that?"
"Absolutely. I searched high and low, but the owner of the apartment clearly didn't believe me. She gave me a really hard time and insisted that I search again, which I did with the same result."
"Right. Well, thanks for your help."
"I wouldn't have minded," he continued. "But that wasn't the end of it. The woman is clearly paranoid."
"Sorry, I don't follow?"
"She called me back there a few days later."
"About the bees?"
"No, this time she insisted that she had woodworm, and

that I had to go straight around there before her floor collapsed."

"What happened?"

"There was no sign of woodworm. I told her it was just a bit of sawdust on the floor. She'd probably brought it in on her shoes."

Chapter 23

It hadn't really occurred to me at the time, but now that I looked back on it, I realised how adamant Gabriella Wilde had been that we should meet in a coffee shop and not at her house. If my hunch was correct, I believed I now knew why she'd been so keen to avoid me paying a visit to her house.

Finding her address proved to be easy enough: She lived in Lower Tweaking, which was a smaller version of Middle Tweaking. Her cottage was set back from the road, and when I drove past, there were no cars parked on the driveway.

I found a quiet, secluded spot just outside the village and parked there. After making myself invisible, I made the short walk back to her cottage. Fortunately, I didn't need to gain access to the house in order to find what I was looking for. Instead, I made my way around the back; the garden was huge and stretched for at least a couple of hundred yards.

Still invisible, I took a slow stroll down the gravel path. To the left was a perfectly manicured lawn, which could have served as a bowling green. To the right was a gorgeous wildflower meadow. In the distance, at the end of the path, was what looked like a large vegetable patch. So far, though, there was no trace of what I'd been hoping to find. Maybe my hunch had been wrong.

But then, as I reached the vegetable patch, I spotted them.

There was little wonder that Gabriella hadn't been fazed by the bees that had so terrified the other members.

Back at the car, I phoned the members of the Washbridge art society. I spoke first to Finley McAdams and asked if he'd be prepared to host a meeting of the society at his house the following afternoon.

Clearly intrigued by my request, he asked the reason for the meeting, but I managed to convince him to wait until everyone was together, at which time I promised all would be revealed. Once he'd agreed, I phoned the others. They weren't particularly enthusiastic at first, but when I told them that if I was unable to arrange a meeting of all the members, I would take my findings to the police, they all eventually agreed. That, in itself, was significant.

A few minutes later, my phone rang. My first thought was that one of the members had had a change of heart, but it turned out to be Swotty Dotty.

"Jill, it's Dorothy. I just wanted to check that you and Jack are still okay for tonight.'

"Absolutely. We're both looking forward to it. We did say eight o'clock, didn't we?"

"That's right. Eight o'clock at Washbridge Tavern. Do you know it?"

"Yeah. It's a long time since I've been there, though. I imagine it'll have changed quite a bit since then."

"Great. We'll see you both tonight."

***

Back at the office, Winky was wearing his black pinstripe suit.

"You're looking very dapper, mister. What's that in aid of?"

"I've been invited to a photoshoot followed by a meal, all paid for by CM Magazine."

"How come they want you and not Trevor the Tails?"

"Trevor will be there too. The first three prize winners in the male and female competitions have all been invited. I'm looking forward to meeting those lovely ladies."

"I bet you are. Where's it being held?"

"In London."

"I can't take you there again today."

"I don't need you to. A chauffeur-driven limousine is being sent for me. I won't be back tonight. They've booked us into a hotel."

"It's alright for some."

I made a call to Jason Bond, the man who now owned the restaurant where Alison Reed had been poisoned.

"Is that Jason?"

"Speaking. Who's that?"

"My name is Sonia Lowe. You don't know me."

"I'm rather busy at the moment, darling. How did you get this number, anyway?"

"I'm a friend of Alison Reed's."

"Like I said, darling, I'm very busy. I don't have time to—"

"I think you'll want to speak to me, Jason. I've just had a visit from a private investigator called Jill Maxwell."

"What did *she* want?"

"She reckons that Alison bought a meal for two on the day she died."

"So what? What's that got to do with me?"

"Maxwell asked if I knew who Alison was seeing that night. I told her that I didn't, but the thing is, Jason, Alison did actually tell me who she was meeting. She said she was seeing you."

"That's rubbish. You don't know what you're talking about, darling."

"In that case, you won't mind if I tell Maxwell and the police what I know."

"Hold on. There's no need to do that, darling. It'll just cause me unnecessary problems over nothing."

"I suppose I could keep the information to myself, but it's going to cost you."

"That's blackmail."

"Not really. I'd call it a mutually beneficial arrangement. You don't want the hassle, and I could do with some extra money."

"How much do you want?"

"Ten grand."

"I'm not giving you that much."

"Fair enough. I guess I'll give Maxwell a call, then."

"Wait! It'll take me a while to get the money together."

"Don't give me that. You're minted."

"I can get it by tomorrow."

"Fair enough. I'll meet you in town."

"No. It has to be somewhere quiet. Do you know the bench on Washbridge Mount?"

"Yeah."

"Right. I'll meet you there tomorrow morning at ten."

***

Jack and I were getting ready for our night out with Swotty Dotty and Ray.

"You did remember to book a taxi, didn't you?" I said.

"I didn't bother. I'm going to drive."

"How come? You won't be able to have a drink."

"I know, but I've got my annual review first thing in the morning, and I don't want to risk turning up with a hangover."

"Are you sure? One drink won't hurt."

"I'd rather not. I'm happy to drive."

"Fair enough. It's probably just as well anyway. If you have a drink, you might forget that Dotty and Ray don't know that you know."

"Don't know that I know what?"

"That I'm a witch, of course."

"Come on, Jill, I've been doing this long enough now. I know the drill. What are those two like anyway?"

"When we were at school, I used to think that Dotty was a real swot."

"I kind of gathered that from her nickname."

"She did so well in the exams that everybody assumed she spent all of her time revising, but it turns out that she barely did any. She used magic to cheat."

"What about him? Ray?"

"He was into every sport imaginable: football, rugby, cricket, track and field, and he was captain of most of the teams."

"A real jock, then." Jack sighed. "If he's like every other jock I've met, he's going to be a real bore."

***

Jack and I arrived at Washbridge Tavern at more or less the same time as Dotty and Ray. It was the first time I'd seen him since I left school, and I couldn't believe my eyes. He was still a good-looking guy, but he'd really let himself go. The last time I'd seen him, he was every inch the athlete, but he'd piled on the pounds since then.

"Hi, Jill," Dotty called when she spotted us. "You remember Ray, don't you?"

"Of course I do." Although there was a lot less of him back then. "This is Jack."

"Very pleased to meet you, Jack. I'm Dorothy."

"How goes it, buddy?" Ray shook Jack's hand.

"Shall we go inside?" Dorothy said. "The table's booked for eight."

The maître d' showed us to a quiet spot at the back of the restaurant where we made small talk for a while until the waiter came to take our order.

"Are you still into sport, Ray?" I asked.

"Not so much these days, as you can probably tell. After I left school, I lost interest. I was too busy going drinking with the boys and dating."

"Until I clipped his wings." Dotty laughed. "You do still play one sport, Ray."

"I guess." He shrugged. "But not everyone would agree that it's a *real* sport."

"Tiddlywinks?" I suggested.

"Actually, I'm really into ten-pin bowling now."

Oh bum!

Jack's face lit up. "That's my sport too, isn't it, Jill?"

"It sure is." Sigh.

"Where do you bowl, Ray?" Jack asked.

"Washbridge Bowl, usually."

"Me too. I'm surprised I haven't seen you there."

"We should have a game sometime."

"Definitely."

Inevitably, the two guys were soon engrossed in a riveting discussion on strikes, spares and the seven-ten split.

"They seem to have hit it off," Dotty said.

"Yeah. Seems like we're both ten-pin bowling widows."

The starters and main course were excellent, and even after the ten-pin bowling conversation had subsided, the four of us still found plenty to talk about. Dotty turned out to be a real hoot, and definitely someone who I'd be happy to meet up with again.

"Anyone for dessert?" Jack called over the waiter.

"I'm very sorry, sir," the waiter said. "I'm afraid that we have to close the restaurant in a few minutes."

"Why's that?" I said.

"There's some kind of problem with the cold-room. The door has frozen shut and we can't get inside. I'm very sorry. I do hope you've enjoyed your meal so far."

"It was excellent," Jack said. "You'd better bring us the bill."

While we waited, and the other three talked, my mind was elsewhere. This was the third restaurant to experience problems with their cold-room in a short period of time, and I had a feeling I knew why.

When we got outside, Dotty and Ray seemed keen to keep the evening going.

"Do you two fancy going onto a club?" Dotty said. "Or we could go back to our place if you like. We can have a drink there."

Jack looked keen, so before he could commit us to anything, I got in quickly.

"We'd love to, Dotty, but Jack has his annual review first thing in the morning, and he needs to be on top form. And, to be honest, I've got a bit of a headache. Could we take a rain check, and make it another night? I've really enjoyed this."

"Of course," Dotty said. "Will you give me a ring?"

"Yeah, I'll do that."

When they'd gone, Jack gave me a puzzled look.

"What was that all about? I wouldn't have minded going back to their place for a while. I would have been okay for the morning."

"I'm sorry, but there's something going on in there that I need to sort out."

"In the restaurant? What kind of *something*?"

I quickly brought him up to speed on the recent cold-room-related incidents, and my suspicions as to their cause.

"Are you saying you think the ice nymphs are inside the cold-room in there?"

"That's my guess. I reckon they take refuge in a different cold-room each night, effectively rendering it useless. The next day, they move on again in order to avoid detection. Daze has been trying to track down these guys for ages."

"Are you going to call her?"

"Not until I'm sure my hunch is correct, and I have them trapped."

"How are you going to trap them?"

"Luckily, I haven't got around to returning these yet." I opened my bag and took out the three tiny traps.

"Those look like miniature versions of the ones you used to catch the wood nymphs."

"They are. I shrank them. And I still have a few pink marshmallows in here too. There should be just enough to bait all three traps."

"How do you know the ice nymphs like pink marshmallows too?"

"I don't. I'll just have to keep my fingers crossed."

"What do you want me to do?"

"There's nothing you can do. You might as well get off home and have a good night's sleep. After I've sorted out these guys, I'll magic myself home."

"Will you be okay?"

"Of course I will. I've already dealt with one set of nymphs this week. Wood nymphs, ice nymphs, they're all the same to me."

"Okay, but promise me you'll be careful."

"Of course I will. You know me, Jack."

After he'd left, I made myself invisible and sneaked back inside the restaurant, where the staff were busy closing up. Once they had turned out the lights and everyone had left, I made my way through to the kitchen. There was no wonder they couldn't get into the cold-room because the door had been transformed into one huge block of ice.

The 'burn' spell made short work of the ice, but it also left a large puddle on the tiled floor. I opened the door, sneaked quietly inside, and listened. Moments later, I heard the familiar inane chatter I was accustomed to hearing from the wood nymphs. After edging a little further inside, I caught a glimpse of two of the despicable creatures. They looked almost identical to the wood nymphs except that these guys had icicles hanging from their limbs, just as Daze had described.

I returned to the door, took out the miniature traps, and restored them to full size. After placing them on the floor, I baited each one with a couple of pink marshmallows. Hopefully, that would be enough.

All I could do now was wait, so I sneaked out of the cold-room and took a seat in the restaurant. The traps had worked very quickly on the wood nymphs, and I was hoping for a similar result tonight.

After an hour, I sneaked back inside the cold-room.

Bingo! All three traps had been sprung. There were two ice nymphs in one trap, and one in each of the others. As soon as they spotted me, they began to yell and scream.

"Let us out of here!"

"How dare you! Let us out!"

"You'll be sorry when we get out of here!"

"The game's up, boys."

I went back through to the restaurant and made a call to Daze.

"Jill?" I could tell by her voice that she was half asleep. "Why are you calling me at this time?"

"It's only just turned ten."

"I was having an early night."

"Sorry, but I think you'll be pleased when I tell you the reason for the call."

"Oh? What's that?"

"You know those ice nymphs you've been trying to track down?"

"Yes?" She suddenly sounded much more awake. "Do you know where they are?"

"Even better than that. I have them trapped."

"You do? That's fantastic. Where are they?"

I gave her the address and she promised she'd be straight over.

Good as her word, she and Blaze appeared a few minutes later. He looked half asleep too. "Where are they, Jill?"

"Follow me." I led the way to the cold-room.

"Wow! Nice work! We've been trying to track these guys down for days."

Chapter 24

The next morning, Jack and I were at the kitchen table, eating breakfast. He'd just finished chewing the last spoonful of his 'yummy' muesli and was staring out of the window.

"It looks like it's going to be a lovely day, Jill. I'm glad that cold snap has finally broken."

"You're very welcome."

"Sorry?"

"I said, 'you're very welcome'. Who do you think is responsible for the end of the cold snap?"

"I know you can be rather full of yourself, but surely even you can't claim to control the weather."

"What do you mean, *full of myself*? And yes, the end of the cold snap is down to me."

"How?"

"How do you think? I got rid of those ice nymphs."

"Daze must have been delighted when you called her."

"Not at first she wasn't because she was in bed, fast asleep. But once she realised that I'd caught the ice nymphs, she soon bucked up. Anyway, how are you feeling about your review this morning?"

"Okay, I guess." He sighed.

"What have you got to be nervous about? You're a good detective."

"Maybe, but you know how it is with reviews. They always seem to find something to criticise."

"You shouldn't take any notice of them. If someone criticises me, it's like water off a duck's back. Not that anyone ever does, obviously."

Just then, my phone rang; it was Aunt Lucy.

"Morning, Jill. I hope you don't mind me calling so early."

"Of course not. There's nothing wrong, is there?"

"No, everything's fine. I just wanted to invite you to a family lunch tomorrow."

"Oh? What's that in aid of? I haven't forgotten someone's birthday, have I?"

"No. It's a celebration for the twins."

"What are they celebrating?"

"They won the Candlefield Businesswoman of the Year award last night."

"Are you sure? The twins?"

"Yes, Jill, of course I'm sure."

"Sorry. How come I wasn't invited to the award ceremony?"

"They probably thought you were too busy. They know how hard you work. Anyway, Grandma has decided we should all have lunch together to celebrate. Can you make it tomorrow?"

"Of course. What time?"

"Midday?"

"Okay, I'll be there."

"What was all that about?" Jack said when I'd finished on the call.

"It was Aunt Lucy. She's invited me over for a family lunch tomorrow. They're celebrating because the twins have won the Candlefield Businesswoman of the Year award."

"Is this some kind of wind-up?" Jack laughed.

"Apparently not. What I don't understand is why they didn't invite me to the ceremony. They normally insist I go everywhere with them."

"Have you said something to upset them?"

"Me? No, I don't think so. I mean, I did laugh when they told me they'd been nominated for the award, but I—"

"That's the reason, then. If they didn't expect to win, they wouldn't want you there in case you ridiculed them even more, would they?"

"You make it sound like I was really horrible to them."

"You were."

"Thanks. Now I feel really bad."

"You'll just have to make it up to them tomorrow."

"I will, yeah. I'll be very supportive."

***

Mrs V was at her desk.

"Good morning, Mrs V. Did you enjoy your time alone without Armi?"

"To tell you the truth, Jill, I didn't. I thought I would, but I missed him dreadfully. The house just didn't seem the same without him."

"Well, he's back now."

"He is and that little trip seems to have done him the world of good."

"In what way?"

"He seems to have finally seen the error of his ways and decided to cut back on his night-time snacking. It was getting ridiculous. Every morning when I got up, at least half a packet of biscuits had gone missing. He must have been eating them after I'd gone to bed. Of course, he denied it, but there's only the two of us in the house, and I definitely hadn't eaten them. But, this morning, the biscuits hadn't been touched, so I'm hoping that marks a new start for him."

"I'm sure it does." And, once again, you're very welcome.

Winky had stayed overnight in London, which meant I could look forward to a nice quiet morning in the office.

Spoke too soon.

There were two cats sitting on the sofa and another two on my desk.

"Hey, you lot. What's going on? What are you doing in here?"

"Hi there." The ginger cat waved a paw at me.

"Never mind, 'hi there'. Why are you lot in my office?"

"It's all above board. We booked it through CatBnB. We've only booked the one night, so we'll be gone in about an hour."

"This office is on CatBnB? Are you sure?"

"Yes. The owner confirmed the booking."

"The *owner*?"

"Yeah."

"What was his name?"

"Winky, I think."

"Right, and you say you'll be gone in an hour?"

"Definitely."

"Okay, but I'm going to need you two to get off my desk. And keep the noise down until you leave."

I was going to have serious words with Winky when he got back. How dare he rent out my office?

***

I was now quietly confident that I knew what had happened to Lori Harty's painting, but if it turned out I was wrong, I was going to have a serious case of egg on my face in a few minutes time when I confronted the members of the Washbridge art society.

Finley McAdams' wife had gone out for the afternoon, so it was Finley himself who answered the door.

"Jill, nice to see you again. The others are in the conservatory. We're all very keen to hear what you have to tell us. I've made iced tea. Will that be okay for you?"

"Iced tea would be lovely, thanks."

Finley led the way to the conservatory where Hannah Westbrook, Myla Donovan and Gabriella Wilde were all chatting. They stopped as soon as I walked into the room.

"Do have a seat, Jill." Finley pointed to one of the wicker chairs near the patio doors. "There's just Lori to wait for now."

"Actually, Finley, she won't be joining us today."

"Why not?"

"Because I didn't tell her about this meeting."

The four of them looked very puzzled by that revelation.

"How come?" Myla said.

"Because it's the four of you that I need to talk to. I think maybe now's the time that you come clean and tell me the truth about what happened to Lori's painting."

"Whatever do you mean?" Gabriella snapped.

"I'm sorry, Jill," Hannah said. "But I have no idea what you're talking about."

"Do you really want to play it this way? Maybe you'd

all prefer I had this conversation with the police."

"There's no need to involve the police." Finley took the chair next to mine. "What is it you think we know?"

"How about you explain why none of you thought to mention that originally all five members of the society had intended to purchase the painting together."

That clearly threw them for a moment, but eventually Hannah spoke up. "So what? We do occasionally combine to purchase a piece. There's nothing particularly unusual about that."

"But isn't it true that the five of you went as far as making an offer to Ethan Porter for The Old Barn?"

"Yes, we did. What of it?"

"As I understand it from Ethan, you offered less than the asking price, and he said he needed time to consider the offer."

"That's true."

"And isn't it also true that in the meantime, Lori took it upon herself to offer Ethan the full asking price, which he duly accepted?"

"That's right, yes," Finley said.

"How did you all feel about that?"

Myla shrugged. "Obviously, we'd have preferred it if she'd told us what she intended to do."

"What about the rest of you?"

"I thought it was a despicable act on her part," Gabriella said.

"I wasn't impressed." Hannah shrugged. "But it's the sort of thing she would do."

"So, it's fair to say that you were all angry. So angry, in fact, that you decided to teach her a lesson."

"I'm sorry, Jill," Finley said. "I really have no idea what

you're getting at. You can't possibly believe that *we* stole the painting. You've seen the CCTV, haven't you? There's no way any one of us could have taken that painting out of the apartment without being seen."

"It's certainly true that you couldn't have taken it out of there in *one* piece, but that's not what happened, is it?" The room fell silent again, and now all four of them shared the same horrified expression. "Lori told me that while she was in the kitchen, making the drinks, she heard a buzzing sound, which she assumed had been the sound of the bees, but it wasn't, Finley, was it?"

"I really don't know what you're getting at."

"I think you do. What Lori actually heard was the sound of your jigsaw — the same one I heard when I came to visit you last time. You used it to cut the painting into two pieces. Each piece just small enough to fit inside a handbag. That's why, later, Lori found traces of sawdust on the floor, which she assumed was the result of woodworm."

"How am I supposed to have taken the jigsaw into the apartment?" Finley said. "It's clear on the CCTV that I wasn't carrying anything."

"Three ladies. Three handbags. Two to carry one half of the painting, and one to carry the jigsaw and a jam jar. Isn't that right, Gabriella?"

"This is preposterous!" she said. "I've a good mind to call my lawyer."

"Please feel free to do just that. And while you're at it, maybe you'd like to explain to him why you took a jar full of bees into the apartment with you. You weren't scared of the bees because they were yours, and you're used to handling them. The glass on the ground below this apartment was from the jam jar, which you threw or dropped from the balcony."

"This is nonsense."

"Is it, though? Really? I was in Washbridge Beekeepers' Sales and Hire yesterday. I saw you in there, looking at protective clothing, I believe."

"Yes, but I — err —"

"How many beehives do you have in your back garden? I counted six."

"Have you been snooping around my house? You had no right to do that."

"Why would we cut a perfectly good painting into pieces?" Myla laughed, nervously.

"I can only think it was out of spite. If you couldn't have it, why should Lori have it?"

"You're right, Jill. About everything," Finley said. The others looked at him in horror, but he continued anyway. "It's no good denying it any longer. We should never have let it go as far as it did. We were just upset."

"What's going to happen now?" Gabriella said. "Are you going to tell Lori and the police?"

"That depends. I happen to think the way Lori went behind your backs was unfair, but that's not to say I condone your actions. I'd rather not involve the police if I don't have to."

"What exactly are you saying, Jill?" Myla said.

"Do you still have the pieces of the painting?"

"I have one back at my place," Hannah said.

"The other one is in the shed," Finley pointed out of the patio doors.

"Right. There's somewhere I have to be when I leave you in a few minutes' time, so I need you to take the two pieces of the painting to my office straight away. I won't be there, but you can leave them with my receptionist. Then, tomorrow, I'll speak to Lori and see if I can smooth things over."

"How on earth are you going to do that?" Finley said. "When she realises what we've done, she'll go ballistic, and she'll insist on bringing in the police."

"Not necessarily. You're just going to have to trust me on this. But, if those two pieces of painting aren't at my office by the time I get back there later today, I'll go straight to the police. Is that clear?"

"Crystal," Finley said.

The others nodded.

"Excellent. In that case, where's that iced tea you promised me?"

***

I'd only ever been able to speak to Jason Bond on the phone. That turned out to be quite fortuitous because it meant I didn't have to bother changing my appearance before presenting myself as Sonia Lowe.

We'd arranged to meet at the bench on top of Washbridge Mount. Thanks to my success in capturing the ice nymphs, I was able to enjoy the sunshine while I waited for Jason to arrive. Had we met in that same spot the previous day, it would have been freezing cold up there.

I'd been there for about ten minutes when I heard footsteps. A well-built man in his mid-thirties, dressed in jeans and a blue T-shirt, was walking towards me. If his expression was anything to go by, he was not in the best of moods.

"Are you Sonia?"

"Jason, how very nice to meet you." It was only when he got closer that I noticed he was wearing gloves. "Have you brought my money?"

"Yeah, I've got it."

I held out my hand.

"Not so fast, darling. Who else have you told that I was meeting Alison?"

"I haven't told anyone."

"How do I know you're telling the truth?"

"You'll just have to take my word for it. Once I have the money, you'll never see or hear from me again."

"I don't believe you. I know your kind, darling. You'll spend this, and then you'll be back for more."

Before I knew it, his hands were around my neck. I should have realised what he had in mind when I spotted the gloves.

He was strong, so I had to act quickly before I blacked out. Using the 'doppelganger' spell, I made myself look like Alison Reed. As soon as he registered my 'new' face, he released his grip on my neck, and stepped back.

"It can't be you." He was freaking out now. "You're dead."

"You don't get rid of me that easily, Jason," I said. "Not after what you did to me. I'm going to haunt you for the rest of your life."

"No, please! I only intended for the poison to make you ill, so that the restaurant would get the blame and be closed down. I didn't mean for it to kill you. It was an accident."

"In that case, why didn't you come forward and admit

your guilt to the police?"

"I was going to, honestly. I thought for sure they'd arrest me, but then they charged that boyfriend of yours with murder."

"Don't come the innocent. You framed Arnold by planting poison at his house."

"No, I didn't. I swear I didn't."

"Tell it to the police."

"Please don't haunt me." He slumped down onto the bench and buried his head in his hands.

I made a call to Sushi who arrived fifteen minutes later, accompanied by two uniformed officers. By then, I'd reversed the 'doppelganger' spell and reverted to my normal appearance.

"What's going on here, Maxwell?" Sushi was out of breath from the climb. "Who's that?" She glanced over at Bond, who was staring at the ground.

"This gentleman is Jason Bond. He killed Alison Reed."

"Who?"

"A young woman who was murdered five years ago. My clients' son, Arnold Kramer, was convicted of her murder and is now serving time in prison."

"What proof do you have that this man was actually the murderer?"

I took the digital recorder from my pocket and played her the exchange I'd had with Jason when he thought I was Alison.

"Why is he calling you by the dead woman's name?" Sushi said.

"I've no idea, but you heard what he said. He was the one who poisoned her."

"You realise we can't use this recording in court."

"I know, but I'm sure if you take Jason in for questioning, he'll be more than happy to give you his confession. Won't you, Jason?"

He looked up. "Where's Alison gone?"

"Alison's dead," I said. "Don't you remember? You poisoned her."

"It was an accident. I didn't mean for her to die. She's not going to come back to haunt me, is she?"

I turned to Sushi. "He's clearly in shock." I handed her the recorder. "You might find this useful, even if you can't use it in evidence."

Sushi told the uniformed officers to take Bond to the police station.

"I'll probably need to speak to you later, Maxwell."

"No problem. You know me. Always pleased to help."

Chapter 25

It didn't matter how many times I helped Sushi, that woman never showed an ounce of gratitude. You would have thought by now, I would have been top of her Christmas card list. Instead, I always came away with the impression that she wished I was the one she was going to lock up. It was time to give the Kramers the good news.

"Mrs Kramer, it's Jill."

"Do you have any news for us?"

"Actually, I do this time."

"Is it good or bad?"

"Good. At least, I think so. Do you know a man called Jason Bond?"

"I don't think so. Should I?"

"He's the current owner of the restaurant where Arnold used to work. The police have just taken him in for questioning, and I'm fairly confident that he's going to confess to the murder of Alison Reed."

"Honestly?" She broke down in tears, and the line went silent for a while, but then Mr Kramer came on. "Jill? What's happened? I can't get any sense out of Elaine."

"I've just told your wife that a man has been taken in for questioning, and I expect him to confess to the murder of Alison Reed."

"Oh, my goodness. That's fantastic. Are you sure, Jill?"

"He's definitely been taken in for questioning, and I'm ninety-nine percent sure that he'll confess to the murder."

"What does that mean for Arnold? Will he be released?"

"If Bond does confess, then yes, but unfortunately these things have a habit of moving rather slowly. I suggest you contact your lawyer. Tell him what's happened and ask him to do everything he can to get the cogs moving as quickly as possible."

"Thank you so very much, Jill. You don't know how much this means to us."

***

Back at the office, Mrs V looked very puzzled indeed.

"Are you all right, Mrs V?"

"Err, yes, dear."

"Are you sure? You look a little confused."

"I am rather. I've had two visitors this afternoon and they both brought in one half of the same painting." She pointed to the two carrier bags on the filing cabinet behind her.

Oh bum!

It had never occurred to me that they'd bring in the two halves of the painting in open bags. I'd assumed they would wrap them up or put them in a box.

Mrs V continued, "They said you'd asked them to bring them in."

"Err, yes, that's right. I did."

"Why on earth would you want a painting that's been cut in half?"

"It's—err— art nouveau. It's been in all the magazines. The artist creates the work and then disassembles it."

"If you say so dear, but it seems rather silly to me."

"I'll take these." I grabbed the bags before Mrs V could ask any more awkward questions.

Winky was lying on the sofa.

"What's in the bags? Salmon, I hope."

"No chance. I have a bone to pick with you, buddy."

"I had an excellent meal last night, and that hotel was top-notch."

"I don't care."

"And Sophia. Darling Sophia. I think I'm in love, Jill."

"Who's Sophia?"

"She came first in the Best Dressed Female competition. She's coming to visit me next week."

"Well, that's all very nice, I'm sure, but what I want to know is how come you've been renting out my office on CatBnB?"

"I thought I'd mentioned that to you."

"No, Winky, you never did. I think I would have remembered."

"It must have slipped my mind."

"How very convenient. When I arrived this morning, there were four cats in here."

"Four? The booking was only for three. The cheek of some people."

"You're the one with all the *cheek*. I don't know how you had the nerve."

"Okay, I'm sorry. I admit I should have mentioned it to you."

"*Sorry*, doesn't cut it. I want fifty percent of the booking fee."

***

"Hello, gorgeous." Jack greeted me at the door with a kiss.

"What do you want?"

"Can't a man give his beautiful wife a kiss when she

gets home from work without having an ulterior motive?"

"Of course he can, but you never do, so you must be up to something."

"Don't be daft. Why don't you go upstairs and get changed while I make you a cup of tea?"

That settled it; he was definitely up to something.

When I came back downstairs, the cup of tea was waiting for me on the kitchen table.

"Put your feet up while I make dinner." He pulled out the chair.

"It's my turn to make it, isn't it?"

"Who's counting? You just enjoy your tea."

"Okay, that's enough. Either you've done something, or you want something. Which is it?"

"That's not very nice. Here am I, just trying to be a loving husband."

"So, which is it?"

"Well — err — "

"I knew it. Come on, you may as well spit it out now."

"Ray called earlier and asked if I wanted to go bowling tomorrow."

"Swotty's Ray?"

"Yeah. I told him we probably had other plans."

"That's okay, then." I took a sip of tea.

"Have we?"

"Have we what?"

"Got other plans?"

"I wish. I have to work tomorrow."

"Great!" He punched the air.

"Charming."

"I didn't mean it's *great* you have to work. That's a

bummer, obviously. But if you do have to work, then I guess I can tell Ray that I'll be able to make it. Unless there's anything you need me to do?"

"Nah. You go and enjoy yourself, but don't sulk when he beats you."

"*Beats me*?" Jack scoffed. "Are you kidding? I'm going to take great pleasure in beating that ex-jock. Are you sure you don't mind me going?"

"Positive. I've got that family lunch tomorrow as well."

"Make sure you're nice to the twins. Don't forget to congratulate them on their award."

"Of course I won't forget. What do you take me for?"

"I'll go and call Ray."

While Jack was on the phone, I went out to the car to get the two sections of painting which I'd left in the boot. I'd just placed them on the kitchen table when Jack came back.

"What's that?"

"What does it look like? It's a painting."

"I can see that, but why is it in halves?"

"It's part of the case I'm working on. This is my client's painting that went missing from her apartment."

"I'm guessing it wasn't in two pieces when it was taken?"

"Correct. I'm trying to figure out how to put it back together again."

"Can't you just magic it back together?"

"You make it sound so easy. I can only repair it if I can figure out which spell to use. I've tried the 'take it back' spell, but no joy. Maybe there'll be something in my spell book. Why don't you start dinner while I try to sort this out?"

I took the two pieces of painting through to the lounge, put them on the coffee table, and then grabbed the spell book. I wasn't optimistic about finding a suitable spell, but as I worked my way through the index, I came across one entitled: *How to Restore a painting which has been cut into three pieces.* That was one more piece than I was dealing with, but I was confident I'd be able to adapt it. The spell in question was part of the premium package, so the money I'd spent on the upgrade hadn't been wasted.

I made a few minor adjustments to the spell, then crossed my fingers, and cast it on the two halves of the painting.

Voilà, it was restored to its former glory.

A few minutes later, Jack joined me. "You did it."

"Piece of cake."

***

Jack and I had moved into the lounge after dinner.

"Hey, Jack, I'm sorry. I totally forgot to ask how your review went this morning."

"It went fine. In fact, the boss was very complimentary."

"See, I told you there was nothing to worry about. Does that mean you'll be in line for a promotion soon?"

"I doubt it. There just aren't the vacancies around here at the moment. I'd probably have to move, and to be honest, I don't fancy doing that."

"You're not just saying that because of me, are you?"

"No. If a chance of promotion comes up around here, I shall apply for it, but in the meantime I'm happy to carry on as I am."

My phone rang.

"Jill, it's Lori Harty. I'm sorry to bother you at home, but I was wondering if you had any news for me?"

"Actually, Lori, I do. I was going to give you a call in the morning, to arrange to come and see you."

"What's the news? Can't you tell me now?"

"To be honest, I'd rather do it face to face."

"Okay. I don't suppose there's any chance you could come around tonight, is there? I know it's cheeky of me to ask, but I go away for the week tomorrow, and I'll be leaving at the crack of dawn. That's why I called this evening."

"Err, okay. I'll be over in about half an hour."

"Who was that?" Jack said when I'd finished on the call.

"It's the client from the missing painting case."

"Are you going over there now?"

"Yeah, she's going away in the morning. I shouldn't be too long."

"What are you going to tell her?"

"That I found her painting in two pieces and used magic to restore it."

"Very funny."

"I'll think of something. I usually do."

***

Lori greeted me at the door, and as soon as she saw the package under my arm, her face lit up.

"Is that what I think it is, Jill?"

"Let's go inside and I'll show you."

I'd wrapped the painting in brown paper, and as soon

as I put it on the kitchen table, she ripped it open. So keen was she to be reunited with her beloved painting.

"You found it!" She gave me a big hug. "Thank you so much. I honestly didn't think I'd ever see it again. Where was it?"

"It was a difficult, complicated investigation, but I eventually managed to track it down to a thief who has been targeting works of art in this area."

"What a terrible person. I hope they lock him up and throw away the key."

"Unfortunately, although I was able to recover your painting, the man got away."

"How annoying."

"The police will catch up with him sooner or later. They always do."

"I can't wait to see the faces of the other members when they see this back on the wall."

I'd pay good money to see that too.

By the time I left Lori's, I was feeling quite peckish, so I gave Jack a call.

"It's me. I've just finished with the client, and I'm really hungry. I thought I might stop off at a takeaway on the way home. Do you fancy anything?"

"Not for me, thanks. I've just had supper."

"Okay, I'll see you later."

I had intended going to the chippy, but on the drive home, I noticed a new takeaway, which sold fried chicken, so I decided to give it a try.

Behind the counter were two men who were clearly brothers.

"Hi," I said. "I haven't noticed this place before."

"We only opened a couple of days ago. I'm Chuck and this is my brother, Ern."

"Do you own this place?"

"We do. We've both worked in the fast-food business for years, but this is the first place of our own. What can I get for you?"

"I'll have some wings please."

"And fries?"

"Yeah, just a small one."

Rather than drive home and risk the food going cold, I sat on one of the stools next to the window to eat my meal. In between serving customers, the two brothers practically told me their life stories.

On my way out, Chuck shouted, "Do call again, Jill."

"Don't worry, I will. That was delicious."

Chapter 26

"Jill, are you okay in there?" Jack shouted from outside the bathroom.

It was the next morning and I'd just spent the last ten minutes throwing up.

"I'm okay."

"Are you sure? Is there anything I can get you?"

"No, honestly, I'm fine now." I managed to get to my feet and make my way out of the bathroom.

"You look terrible," he said.

"Thanks, buddy."

"I'll give Ray a call and tell him I can't make it today."

"Don't be silly. I'm feeling much better now. It must have been that takeaway I had last night. I really enjoyed it too, but I can't think what else it could be. I definitely won't be calling there again, that's for sure."

"Are you positive you don't want me to stay at home with you?"

"There's no point. I won't be here anyway. There are things I have to do today."

"Why don't you take the day off?"

"I can't. There's somewhere I have to go this morning on business, and I've got that family lunch at Aunt Lucy's. Although, to be honest, I'm not sure I'll feel much like eating."

An hour later, I'd showered and dressed, and was feeling one hundred percent better. I'd even managed to keep down some tea and toast.

I'd practically had to throw Jack out of the door because he didn't want to leave me alone, but as I kept pointing out, I was going out anyway.

***

As I drove into Middle Tweaking, I noticed that Myrtle's house was now under offer. Boy, that was a quick sale, but then the old watermill was a lovely property, so I shouldn't really have been surprised.

But I wasn't here to see Myrtle today.

Walter Staniforth was clearly surprised to see me again so soon.

"Jill, you'll have the villagers talking about us if you keep popping over so often." He laughed.

I wasn't in the mood for his humour. "Do you think I could come in, Walter?"

"Of course. Is everything alright? You seem rather serious today."

"There's something I need to talk to you about, and it would be better said inside."

"You'd better come in, then. Can I get you a cup of tea or coffee?"

"No, thanks." Once we were in the lounge, I got straight down to business. "Walter, I thought you should know that another man has now confessed to the murder of Alison Reed."

"Oh?"

"His name is Jason Bond. He owns the restaurant where Arnold Kramer worked at the time of Alison Reed's death."

"And how do you know all of this, Jill?"

"Because I was the one who handed him over to the police."

"You do realise that he'll probably turn out to be some kind of nutjob, don't you? People confess to all kinds of things all the time."

"That's probably true, but that isn't the case this time. He's admitted he was with Alison on the night she died, and that he slipped the poison onto her food. At the time of the murder, he owned a competing restaurant a few miles away. The thing is, he never actually intended to kill her; he just expected her to become ill. He was banking on the bad publicity having an adverse effect on the restaurant. Unfortunately, he badly misjudged the amount of poison needed, and instead of making her ill, she died."

"If that's true, then that is indeed a tragedy."

"Not just for Alison. Arnold Kramer is a victim here too. He's spent the last five years behind bars for a crime he didn't commit."

"You're right, Jill. That is unfortunate, but if this other guy turns out to be the murderer, I'm sure Kramer will be released soon enough."

"But it should never have happened, Walter, and it wouldn't have done, but for you."

"Hold on, Jill. That's rather harsh. Perhaps mistakes were made, but we carried out a thorough investigation."

"This miscarriage of justice is not the result of *mistakes*. The moment you identified Arnold Kramer as the prime suspect, you made it your business to ensure he was convicted."

"I did my job if that's what you mean."

"You did much more than that, Walter. You framed Arnold Kramer."

"That's an outrageous thing to say." He was red in the face now. "How dare you?"

"At the time of the murder, you were coming up to retirement. Naturally, you wanted to go out on a high. Finding Alison Reed's murderer ensured you would do that."

"What exactly are you accusing me of?"

"Well, for starters, you blackmailed Karen Little into perjuring herself. She never saw Arnold threaten Alison."

"That is absolute nonsense. If she told you that, she's a liar."

"That's not the worst of it, Walter. The most damning evidence against Arnold Kramer was the poison found at his house."

"I'm well aware of that. I was the senior investigating officer on the case, remember."

"Jason Bond was quite prepared to admit to the murder of Alison Reed, and yet he was adamant that he hadn't planted the poison at Kramer's house. Why would he bother to deny that when he'd just confessed to the worst of all crimes? There can be only one reason: he didn't plant the poison. Someone else did. Someone who had unrestricted access to the murder scene. The lead detective, for example."

"How dare you suggest such a thing?" He stood up. "I'd like you to leave now. I won't sit here and allow you to slander me in this way."

"Gladly." I stood up. "But I must tell you that I plan to pass all of this information to the police."

"And do you really think they'll take your word over that of an esteemed retired colleague?"

"Maybe, maybe not, but I intend to do everything in my power to make sure that they do, and that you are punished for the terrible thing you did to Arnold

Kramer."

As he practically pushed me out the door, the look on his face was no longer one of anger. It was one of fear.

***

It was about ten minutes before midday when I magicked myself over to Aunt Lucy's house. Knowing how tardy the twins usually were, I expected to arrive before them, so I was rather surprised to find Amber and Pearl already seated in the dining room with Aunt Lucy and Grandma.

"Isn't Martin coming?" I said.

"He was invited but he never got back to us," Grandma grumbled. "Are you going to sit down? You're making the place look untidy."

"Sorry." I took the seat directly opposite her.

Before we started on the meal, I thought I should try to make amends to the twins for having mocked their award nominations.

"Amber, Pearl, I just wanted to say congratulations on winning the award. It's definitely well-deserved."

And yes, I did somehow manage to say that with a straight face.

The two of them began to giggle; that definitely wasn't the reaction I'd expected. I thought they'd be pleased that I'd complimented them.

"What are you two laughing at?"

"The twins didn't actually win an award," Aunt Lucy said.

"Oh? But you told me they had."

"There's no such thing as the Candlefield

Businesswoman of the Year award," Grandma said.

"Now I'm totally confused. If we aren't here to celebrate the twins' award, why are we here?"

"The real reason we're here, Jill," Grandma said, "is to celebrate the soon-to-be new addition to our family."

"Oh?" I glanced over at the twins. "Amber? Pearl? Not both of you, again?"

"It's not us," Amber said.

"Then I'm sorry, but I don't understand."

"This celebratory lunch is for you, Jill," Grandma said. "You're the one who will soon be introducing a new member into our family."

I laughed. "Is this some kind of wind-up?" I could tell by Grandma's expression that she was deadly serious. "You bring me over here under false pretences, and then you try to tell me that I'm—. That's ridiculous. I think I would know."

"You have been eating some strange stuff recently," Amber said.

"Yeah, and you've totally gone off blueberry muffins," Pearl chipped in.

"So, let me get this right. You're basing this nonsense on the fact that I've gone off blueberry muffins, are you?"

"You've gone off custard creams too," Aunt Lucy said.

"Unbelievable."

"Have you been feeling sick in the mornings, Jill?" Grandma said.

"Sick? Err, no, I haven't. Of course, I haven't. This is too much." I stood up. "I'm leaving."

"Don't go, Jill," Aunt Lucy said. "Stay for lunch."

"I'm sorry, Aunt Lucy, but I don't want to listen to any more of this nonsense."

And with that, I magicked myself back to Washbridge city centre.

I was absolutely livid. How dare they spring something like that on me? And how had they managed to put two and two together to get five like that?

I'd show them.

I popped into the first pharmacy that I came across and bought one of those testing kit things. I would take it home, do the test, and then magic myself back to Candlefield, to show them all just how ridiculous they were being.

***

I was in the lounge, staring at the little blue cross. This couldn't be happening.

But it was.

How had I not realised? There had been so many signs. Not just the change in my appetite and the bout of sickness; there had been other clues too, but I'd put them all down to stress. I'd been working so hard recently.

I almost jumped out of my skin when my phone rang.

"Jill, it's Martin."

"Hi. I thought you might have been at Aunt Lucy's earlier."

"I couldn't make it. I'm calling because there's something very important that I have to tell you. But first, I should say congratulations."

"You know, then?"

"Yes, your grandmother told me."

"It seems like everyone knew except me. I feel like such a fool."

"Don't be silly. You are pleased, aren't you?"

"Of course I am. I'm still in shock, that's all. Anyway, where have you been hiding?"

"Something unexpected cropped up, and it means I won't be able to see you again."

"For how long?"

"Forever, probably."

"What do you mean? You've only just come into my life. You can't just disappear again."

"I have no choice. I'm really sorry. I honestly thought he was dead."

"Who?"

"He had me fooled, Jill. He had everyone fooled. He's not dead, so I have to stay here to try to keep your child safe."

"I don't understand. What are you talking—" He'd hung up, so I called him straight back, but the line was dead. Number unknown.

This day had just gone from crazy to totally insane.

***

When Jack arrived home, he was full of smiles.

"I told you I'd beat that ex-jock, didn't I?" That's when he saw the look on my face. "Jill, what's wrong? Have you been sick again? Why didn't you call me if you were feeling unwell?"

"It's not that. I'm okay."

"What's wrong, then?"

I held up the indicator stick.

"What's that?" He took it from me. "Is this what I think it is?"

I nodded.

"You're—?"

"Apparently. I found out from Grandma."

"From your grandmother? How did she know?"

"Who knows?"

He pulled me into his arms and gave me a hug. "I love you so much."

"I love you, too." I managed through my tears.

Then, without warning, he let me go, disappeared out of the room, and hurried upstairs.

Had the shock been too much for him? Was he going to be sick now?

I found him in the spare bedroom, dismantling the train set, and throwing the pieces into a big box.

"Jack, what are you doing?"

"Clearing this out to make room for the nursery."

"But you'll break your train set."

"Who cares? All that matters now is you and me." He came over and put his hand on my tummy. "And this little one."

ALSO BY ADELE ABBOTT

The Witch P.I. Mysteries
(A Candlefield/Washbridge Series)

Witch Is When... (Season #1)
Witch Is When It All Began
Witch Is When Life Got Complicated
Witch Is When Everything Went Crazy
Witch Is When Things Fell Apart
Witch Is When The Bubble Burst
Witch Is When The Penny Dropped
Witch Is When The Floodgates Opened
Witch Is When The Hammer Fell
Witch Is When My Heart Broke
Witch Is When I Said Goodbye
Witch Is When Stuff Got Serious
Witch Is When All Was Revealed

Witch Is Why... (Season #2)
Witch Is Why Time Stood Still
Witch is Why The Laughter Stopped
Witch is Why Another Door Opened
Witch is Why Two Became One
Witch is Why The Moon Disappeared
Witch is Why The Wolf Howled
Witch is Why The Music Stopped
Witch is Why A Pin Dropped
Witch is Why The Owl Returned
Witch is Why The Search Began
Witch is Why Promises Were Broken
Witch is Why It Was Over

Witch Is How... (Season #3)
Witch is How Things Had Changed
Witch is How Berries Tasted Good
Witch is How The Mirror Lied
Witch is How The Tables Turned
Witch is How The Drought Ended
Witch is How The Dice Fell
Witch is How The Biscuits Disappeared
Witch is How Dreams Became Reality
Witch is How Bells Were Saved
Witch is How To Fool Cats
Witch is How To Lose Big
Witch is How Life Changed Forever

Witch Is Where... (Season #4)
Witch is Where Magic Lives Now

Susan Hall Investigates
(A Candlefield/Washbridge Series)
Whoops! Our New Flatmate Is A Human.
Whoops! All The Money Went Missing.
Whoops! Someone Is On Our Case.
Whoops! We're In Big Trouble Now.

Murder On Account (A Kay Royle Novel)

Web site: AdeleAbbott.com
Facebook: facebook.com/AdeleAbbottAuthor

Printed in Great Britain
by Amazon

41128884R00158